"You okay?" Nikolai leaned close, looked into her eyes.

Her vision was still blurry, and the angles and planes of his face seemed to shift and sway as she tried to meet his gaze. Or maybe it was the tears swimming in her eyes that made it seem that way.

"I'm sorry, Jenna. There was nothing you could have done to save her. You know that, right?"

"I know that my head hurts. I know that I'm more tired than I've ever been in my life. I know that I wish I'd never agreed to go on that mission trip." But she didn't know that what Nikolai was saying was true. Maybe she'd missed an opportunity. Maybe she could have done something that would have changed things.

"Jenna—"

"I hate crying in front of strangers," she said.

"I don't think we're strangers anymore," he responded, and the first tear slipped down Jenna's cheek. He wiped it away.

Books by Shirlee McCoy

Love Inspired Suspense   **Steeple Hill Trade**

*The Sinclair Brothers
**Heroes for Hire

SHIRLEE MCCOY

has always loved making up stories. As a child, she daydreamed elaborate tales in which she was the heroine—gutsy, strong and invincible. Though she soon grew out of her superhero fantasies, her love for storytelling never diminished. She knew early that she wanted to write inspirational fiction, and she began writing her first novel when she was a teenager. Still, it wasn't until her third son was born that she truly began pursuing her dream of being published. Three years later she sold her first book. Now a busy mother of five, Shirlee is a homeschool mom by day and an inspirational author by night. She and her husband and children live in Washington and share their house with a dog, two cats and a bird. You can visit her website at www.shirleemccoy.com, or email her at shirlee@shirleemccoy.com.

RUNNING BLIND

Shirlee McCoy

Steeple
Hill®

Published by Steeple Hill Books™

STEEPLE HILL BOOKS

Steeple
Hill®

Recycling programs
for this product may
not exist in your area.

ISBN-13: 978-0-373-44416-8

RUNNING BLIND

Copyright © 2010 by Shirlee McCoy

www.SteepleHill.com

Printed in U.S.A.

In that day the deaf will hear the words of the scroll, and out of gloom and darkness the eyes of the blind will see. Once more the humble will rejoice in the Lord; the needy will rejoice in the Holy One of Israel.

—*Isaiah* 29:18,19

To Brenda Minton, Love Inspired author, friend, sister of the heart. Of all the things that being a writer has brought into my life, I value your friendship the most.

ONE

Jenna Dougherty woke to darkness, the pulsing agony in her head drowning out sound, wiping away thoughts and memories. For a moment she knew nothing but darkness, nothing but pain, and then she knew it all.

Three men breaking down the door to the hotel room, dragging Magdalena Romero away. Jenna following, screaming for help as she tried to save her friend. Both of them being shoved into a van and driven for hours before being dumped into a basement room.

Had they been there days or hours before the men had returned? Jenna wasn't sure, she only knew that she and Magdalena had fought for freedom.

Fought and lost.

For Jenna, there had been a moment of agony, and then nothing.

Until now.

Jenna tried to move her arms and legs, tried to call out, but the bonds were too tight, the rag over her mouth oily and old. She gagged, her heart racing with terror, her fingers scratching against dirt-covered cement as she tried to gain leverage and mobility. She twisted onto her side, trying to shimmy closer to the area where she'd last seen Magdalena. Was she still there? Or had she been taken?

Please, God, let her still be here.

A sound drifted through the darkness. Fabric rustling as someone moved. Soft footfalls on cement.

Jenna tensed, her eyes straining in the darkness. She saw nothing, not even a hint of light or movement, but the blackness seemed to pulse with energy. Someone *was* there. She felt what she could not see, and she braced for the attack she knew was coming.

A humid breeze tickled her cheeks, carrying a hint of rain and the dusty, thick scent of sun-baked earth. Was a door open? A window?

She needed to get her numb hands moving, try to undo the heavy rope that bound her. Only then would she have a chance at survival. She shifted, hoping to ease the pressure on her arms, get some blood flowing to her fingers. She *could* do this. She *would*.

The sound came again. Closer. Maybe only feet away, then right beside her. The air alive with it. Someone touched her neck—warm, dry fingers probing the pulse point there—and Jenna jerked back.

Or tried to.

Her movements were sluggish, the retreat nothing more than a subtle recoiling of muscle.

"It's okay. I'm here to help." The voice was as deep and velvety as the darkness, but Jenna didn't believe the lie. She wanted to kick and punch and claw her way to freedom, but her body would not respond, and she could do nothing but lie still as hands slid down her arms, felt the rope around her wrists.

"I'm going to use a knife to cut you free, Jenna. Hold still. Your brother will have my hide if I hurt you."

Her brother?

Kane? Had their folks called him when she hadn't made her Monday evening phone call?

She tried to ask, but the gag kept her from speaking, and she choked on the oily cloth.

A hand smoothed her hair, the cold blade of a knife pressing close to her head for just a second before the gag fell away.

"I—" she started, but her mouth was dry, her throat tight, and she could do nothing but suck in great gulps of humid air until she thought she would drown in it.

"Shhhhh. Whatever needs to be said can be said when we're out of here." He spoke quietly, his hand gentle on her cheek. There and gone as he bent over her wrists, sliced through the ropes. Her ankles were next, and then she was free but not free, her body still numb from hours spent tied up.

"Can you stand?"

"Yes." If it meant escaping, she could do anything. She pushed against the floor, struggled to her knees.

His arm wrapped around her waist, and he pulled her upright. "Come on. We may be on borrowed time."

"I can't leave my friend," Jenna rasped out. "Magdalena?"

"There's no one here. Just us."

"She was here. She has to *still* be here." Jenna took a step away, her legs trembling, sharp pain shooting up from her feet as the blood began flowing there again.

"There's no one here. Let's go before that changes."

"It's dark. Maybe if we find a light…"

"What did you say?" He put a hand on her shoulder, holding her still.

"We need to turn on the light."

Fabric rustled and hands cupped her cheeks.

"What can you see, Jenna?"

She wanted to shove his hands away, tell him that they had more to worry about than what she could or couldn't see, but something in his tone held her motionless. "Nothing."

"No shadows? No light?"

"No."

"It's broad daylight. There's light spilling in from the window I climbed in through. You can't see it?"

She went cold at his words, everything within her stilling.

And then she reached up, touched her eyes, not sure what she expected to feel. What she hoped to feel. Maybe a blindfold. Something that would be blocking the light. But there was nothing.

"I can't see anything."

"You've got a deep bruise on your forehead. Maybe that has something to do with it." His fingers traced a line from the bridge of her nose to her hairline, probing the tender flesh there.

"It doesn't matter how it happened. I'm blind!" She could feel herself panicking, feel the breath catching in her throat, her mind spinning away.

"Hey, it's okay. Take a deep breath. Let it out slowly." He laid his palm against her cheek again, let it rest there as she tried to catch her breath.

"No. It's not."

"Yeah. It is. You're alive, and you're going to stay that way. We'll worry about the rest after we're out of here."

He was right.

She needed to calm down, get a handle on her emotions the same way she had the day she'd been told she had cancer and had less than a year to live. She'd fought that diagnosis, and she'd won. This was simply another battle, another challenge.

"Okay. I'm okay," she managed to say, even though she wasn't sure it was true.

"I knew you were. Now, let's get out of here and get you to a hospital." There was a hint of an accent to his voice, but Jenna couldn't place it.

"We have to find Magdalena first." She pulled away, turning around in a circle, the darkness suddenly deeper, more oppressive. She was blind, and that was something she couldn't think about. Not if she was going to help her friend and herself.

"I told you, she's not here."

"Then they took her. We have to figure out where they brought her." She took a step, her arms out in front of her as she tried to navigate her way through the blackness.

"How? Who would we ask? The men who beat you? We don't know what happened to your friend. Maybe she's alive. Maybe she's not. What we know is that you *are* alive, and if you're going to stay that way, we've got to get out of here."

Maybe she's alive.

Maybe she's not.

The words slammed into Jenna's already pounding head. She and Magdalena had met in college and become good friends. Jenna had been Magdalena's maid of honor when she'd gotten married and had been on hand for the birth of her son three years ago. When Jenna was diagnosed with leukemia, Magdalena had left her busy Houston medical practice and flown to New York to be by her side.

They weren't just friends; they were sisters.

And there was no way Jenna was going to leave Mexico without her.

She yanked away from her rescuer's hold and ran, arms stretched out, feeling through the darkness. Her feet tangled in something, and she tripped, momentum carrying her forward too quickly for her sluggish body to compensate. She went down hard, her hands and knees sliding across concrete, pain stabbing up her arms.

Hot tears slid down her cheeks and she didn't have the strength to wipe them away. Didn't have the strength to get up and run again.

She caught a whiff of leather and mint, felt a warm palm brush the moisture from her cheeks, the touch so tender and light, so filled with compassion that more tears burned behind her eyes.

"You're in no condition to hunt for your friend. Do you see that now?" His voice rumbled through the darkness, steely and hard, much different from the gentleness of his touch.

Jenna stiffened, struggled to her feet, wishing she had the strength to prove him wrong. "You've made your point."

"I don't have a point. I have a goal, and that's to get you back home alive."

"What about Magdalena? She's got a little boy." All Jenna had was a black cat named Dante who came and went as he pleased.

"I know."

"Then leave me here and go find her. I'll be safe enough until—"

"Shh. Someone is upstairs." He pressed a finger to her lips, and she froze, listening as a floorboard creaked above her head.

"We need to get out of here. Come on." He swooped her up, carrying her across the room and setting her down again almost before she realized what he was doing.

"There's a window high up on the wall. I'll climb out, make sure the area is secure and then pull you through. Okay?" He whispered against her ear, his breath ruffling her hair.

There was a whisper of noise, and she knew she was alone again.

A minute ticked by. Then another.

Or maybe just seconds had passed, the darkness and ominous silence stretching each second into minutes, each minute into hours.

Floorboards creaked again, the sound reverberating through the tomblike basement.

Would the door fly open?

Would men pound down the stairs and haul Jenna away, just as they had Magdalena?

She reached forward and touched cement blocks, ran her palms up the rough surface, unwilling to wait another second for her rescuer to pull her through the window. Splintered wood dug into the palm of her hand, but she didn't pull back.

The windowframe. It had to be.

It was high. Maybe two feet above her head, but not so high that she couldn't manage to pull herself up and out. She felt along the wood with both hands, running her palms to the edge of the frame and as high as she could on either side. It was large enough to escape through, and she boosted herself up, ignoring the pain as slivers of wood pierced her skin.

If there was broken glass, she didn't feel it as she maneuvered her shoulders through the opening, felt hot sun bathe her face and realized her mistake. Was she at ground level? Or higher? Was anyone watching her escape? Was her rescuer standing nearby, or had he run?

She didn't know, but she was fully committed to her escape, and she wasn't going to back down now. She reached forward, trying to feel the ground, and shrieked as someone grabbed her hand.

"Shh. Do you want whoever's hanging out in that house to come after us?" her rescuer hissed.

"You could have warned me you were there."

"I was trying to maintain silence for the safety of both of us." He grabbed her other hand, tugged gently. "The ground is two inches below you. Come on. Let's get moving."

He gave another tug and Jenna maneuvered the rest of the way out the window. Humid air enveloped her, filling her nose with the scent of sun-baked earth and rotting garbage. Somewhere in the distance, people were talking or arguing, their rapid-fire Spanish beyond what Jenna was able to understand. Aside from that, the day was silent. No hum of traffic. No roar of buses. Nothing like the bustling Mexican border town where Jenna and Magdalena had been working with Team Hope.

"Where are we?" she whispered, as her rescuer urged her forward.

"Santo Trista. It's twenty miles from the border. Now, how about we stay quiet until we're in my car and out of here? I don't like the feel of things."

Neither did Jenna.

As a matter of fact, every hair on the back of her neck was standing on end.

Somewhere behind them, a voice called out, the Spanish words faint and unintelligible.

Her rescuer tensed, his hand tightening on Jenna's. She could feel him shifting position. Was he looking for the source, searching for some sign of what was to come?

A loud crack split the silence, and Jenna screamed, the sound cut off as she was lifted, thrown over a shoulder. Her head bounced against warm leather, the jarring motion only adding to the throbbing agony in her head.

They were moving fast, and she could hear her rescuer's steady, deep breaths as he covered ground. He was in shape, she'd give him that, but Jenna doubted that was going to be enough to save them. Another sharp crack, and something whizzed by so close that Jenna felt it slice through the air.

She wanted to scream. *Would* have screamed, but her throat was too tight with fear.

Please, God, please.

The prayer was only half-formed when her rescuer skidded to a stop, shifted her weight. "In. Quick."

He slid her down in front of him, and she reached out blindly, her hands sliding against warm leather seats as her rescuer urged her to move.

And she did. Crawling onto the leather seat, barely managing to move aside as he climbed in after her. The engine roared to life, and the vehicle jerked forward, picking up speed at an alarming rate.

"Get down!" He shouted the order as he pressed a hand against her back, forcing her to lean forward, her head slamming into something as she went. Pain wiped away all thought, and for a moment she floated in darkness, hearing nothing, feeling nothing. Glass shattered, dragging her from the edge of unconsciousness, pulling her back into reality.

She tried to sit up but was pressed back down as the car continued to accelerate, the tires spinning as her rescuer took another sharp turn. Jenna flew sideways, banging into the door and bouncing back again. She gripped the seat, her fingers digging into soft leather.

Had she escaped the basement so that she could die in a fiery crash?

Please, God, get me out of this alive.

The prayer filled her mind as the car took another sharp turn. She lost her grip on the seat, flew into the door again, her shoulder hitting first, her head following. Pain exploded through her and she felt a brief moment of panic, and then she felt nothing at all.

TWO

Nikolai Jansen had survived enemy fire in Afghanistan and a roadside bomb in Iraq. He didn't plan to die twenty miles from the U.S. border during what should have been an easy assignment.

He took a sharp left, smiling grimly as the squeal of tires and the sound of shattering glass filled the car. The old truck that had been following hadn't been able to make the turn.

Good.

One less carload of bad guys to deal with.

Beside him, Jenna groaned, straightening in her seat and nearly toppling forward into the dashboard. He grabbed her shoulder, holding her up as he eased off the accelerator. She was in bad shape. Beaten and blind, the wound on her forehead three different shades of green and blue. The sooner he got her to a hospital the better, but stopping now wasn't an option. The Mexican drug cartel that had grabbed her was notorious for silencing people it took issue with. It seemed that Jenna was one of them. Or, perhaps, it had simply been her friend the Mexican Panthers were after.

"Did we lose them?" Her words were soft and slurred, her face colorless, aside from the bruise on her forehead and the freckles that dotted her nose and cheeks. According to her brother, Nikolai's boss, Kane Dougherty, she'd been in Mexico working as a physical therapist at a pediatrics clinic. She hadn't gotten anything but trouble for her effort.

"For now."

"What if they find us again?"

"Let's not borrow trouble."

"I'm not talking about borrowing it. I'm talking about having it handed to us on a silver platter," she muttered, leaning her head back against the seat.

"If they find us again, we'll deal with it the way we did before."

"By running?"

"Or fighting. Whichever will get us out of the situation alive."

"I'm not sure I'm in great shape for fighting."

"No worries. I've got enough fight in me for both of us."

"You said my brother sent you."

"I work for your brother's PI firm and was following a lead in San Antonio. Kane asked if I could take a trip across the border to see how you were doing."

"Typical Kane. Always keeping an eye on the people he loves."

"That's not such a bad thing, is it?" he asked, more to keep Jenna talking than because of any real need for conversation. Twenty minutes and they'd hit the U.S. border and the medical help Jenna obviously needed. Twenty minutes wasn't long in the grand scheme of a life, but with head injuries, twenty minutes could be all a person had.

"No. And, right at this moment, I'm really glad he likes to keep an eye on me. I couldn't have escaped that basement without your help." She paused, took a deep shaky breath. "I don't suppose you have any kind of pain relievers on you?"

"There's a bottle of Tylenol in your purse, but I'm not sure a doctor would approve of you having any."

"You've got my purse?" Her head was tilted down and her hair fell forward, covering her face and preventing him from seeing her expression.

He reached over and brushed straight red hair from her forehead and cheek, and she turned her head, her light blue eyes eerily empty. Blind, she'd said, and looking in her blank stare, Nikolai had no doubt that she was right.

"*Do* you have my purse?" she repeated, and Nikolai jerked his attention back to the road and to the conversation. He'd have time to feel sorry for Jenna after they made it to safety. Until then, all his focus needed to be on the mission.

"I grabbed it from your hotel room. I figured you might need your passport and ID." And he'd also figured that if the police found the purse, they'd keep it until Jenna or a family member retrieved it. That would have made it difficult for him to follow through on his plan to find Jenna and to get her out of Mexico.

"I guess your foresight paid off."

"It will if we make it to the border."

"How far are we from it?"

"Fifteen minutes." But it only took seconds for things to change. For good to turn bad. For easy to become difficult. He'd seen it dozens of times as a Marine in Iraq and Afghanistan. Had nearly died when a peaceful day had exploded into violence. Expecting the unexpected was what he'd been trained to do. Returning to the United States and to life as a civilian hadn't changed that.

"Fifteen minutes. That's not so bad, and I guess if we've made it this far, there's no reason to think we won't make it the rest of the way," she said.

He didn't bother to tell her that there was *every* reason to think they wouldn't. There was no point in stating the obvious. "Once I get you across the border, I'll go back and search for your friend."

"If that's what you're planning, why cross the border at all? We can both go look for her." Her voice was weak, the adrenaline that had been keeping her going, fading.

"We've covered that ground before, Jenna. Right now, my priority is you."

"Because my brother is paying the tab? If that's the case—"

"No one is paying the tab. I came down here as a favor to a friend."

"Then let's go back. Magdalena—"

"Wouldn't want you to die for her."

At his words, she fell silent, dropping her head into her hands, her thoughts about his comment hidden. Either she realized the truth of his words, or she'd run out of energy and no longer had the strength to argue.

Nikolai wanted to comfort her, but there was nothing he could say. No way that he could convince her that they were doing the right thing. Leaving someone behind never felt right, regardless of the circumstances.

He pulled his cell phone from his pocket and dialed Kane Dougherty's number. Owner of Information Unlimited, Kane had asked Nikolai to join the private investigative firm two months ago. The job offer had come at the right time, and Nikolai had accepted. Since then, he'd tracked down missing relatives for two clients, traced the money trail of a man who'd left his wife and kids for another woman, and followed a suspected embezzler from Houston to San Antonio.

And now he'd found Kane's sister bound and gagged in the stronghold of the Mexican Panthers.

"Dougherty here."

"Are you still in the States?"

"In Denver. I've got a three-hour layover here. I'll be in Mexico at three. Do you have any news?"

"Better than news. I've got your sister. We're a couple of miles from the border."

"Is she okay?"

"She's injured."

"How badly?"

"She's blind."

Dougherty didn't respond, his silence speaking volumes. He was worried about his sister. Desperate to be there to protect her. Frustrated because he wasn't. Nikolai understood all those feelings. He'd felt them all in the twenty years during which he'd been separated from his sisters. He'd been blessed to be reunited with Morgan, but Katia was still out in the world somewhere. An adult now, but still his little sister and still, in some indefinable way, his responsibility.

"Tell him I'm okay." Jenna roused herself enough to speak, and Dougherty must have heard.

"Is that her? Let me speak to her."

"Are you up to speaking with your brother?" Nikolai asked, and Jenna nodded.

He placed the phone in her palm, felt her hand trembling. She was still terrified and probably in shock, her skin cool and clammy to the touch. He should have grabbed the blanket he kept in the trunk of the car and wrapped it around her shoulders, but there hadn't been time for anything but getting her in the car and getting her out of the line of fire.

"Kane? No, I can't see anything, but I'm sure it's not permanent." There was confidence in her voice, and Nikolai wondered if she really believed what she was saying or if she was simply trying to reassure her brother.

He didn't ask, just took the phone after she finished her conversation and tucked it into his pocket. The border checkpoint was just ahead. Several cars were waiting to pass through, and Nikolai pulled into line behind them.

"We've slowed down. What's going on?" Jenna asked, her voice much weaker than it had been when she'd spoken to her brother. Her lips and face were colorless, the bruise on her forehead deep purple.

"We're at the border."

"Then I guess we're home free." There was no relief in her voice, no indication that she was happy to be within reach of safety.

Was she thinking about Magdalena?

Or had she realized that making it to the border and making it across were two different things?

Nikolai didn't ask. Just inched the car forward, his gaze on a car pulling up behind him. It looked like any other car, and maybe it was, but the hair on the back of Nikolai's neck stood on end, his pulse thrumming. Danger hung in the air, and he couldn't ignore it.

He turned the steering wheel, maneuvering out of line, and speeding toward the border checkpoint.

"What's happening?" Jenna's panicked cry mixed with the roar of the engine, but Nikolai didn't have time to answer. The doors of the other vehicle opened, and two men climbed out.

"Get down!" He shouted the command, and Jenna obeyed, diving down as the first bullet exploded through the rear window. Another followed, the sound reverberating through the car as Border Patrol agents streamed from their stations. Nikolai slammed on his brakes, the tires squealing as the car shuddered to a stop.

"Are w—" Jenna started to rise, and Nikolai shoved her down again, throwing his body over hers.

Gunfire blasted around them, the sound blocking out everything but the thundering beat of Nikolai's heart.

For a moment he was in Afghanistan again, diving for cover as the enemy fired from a rooftop. He could smell the dirt and the coppery scent of his comrades' blood, could hear his own desperate prayers rising from the deepest part of his soul.

And then there was silence, and he was back in the present, pressing Jenna down into leather seats, smelling flowery shampoo and fear.

Jenna tried to move, but he held her down. "Wait another minute. Let's give everyone time to calm down. We don't want to get shot by the good guys."

"Right." She panted the word, and he shifted his weight, trying to give her room to breathe. He could feel her trembling, could hear the quick, sharp intake of air as she struggled not to panic.

"It's okay. Everything is going to be fine," he said quietly, smoothing deep red hair from her cheek. Her skin was silky and much too cool for such a warm day.

"You. In the car. Sit up slowly. Keep your hands where we can see them." The shouted command was repeated in Spanish, and Nikolai did as he was told, rising slowly, his hands in the air.

Jenna did the same, swaying slightly as she moved.

Nikolai wanted to put a hand on her shoulder and hold her steady, but he doubted he'd live long enough to regret it if he did.

The car doors opened, and Nikolai was dragged out.

"Watch out for my friend. She's got a head injury, and she can't see. We need to get her medical attention," he said as the patrol officer frisked him.

"Let's take things slow. Why don't you tell me who you are and why you've got someone gunning for you?" The officer took a step back, allowing Nikolai to turn around and face him. A body lay on the road a few yards away, and another gunman was being frisked by a border patrol officer.

"I'm Nikolai Jansen. My friend was kidnapped and held prisoner by the Mexican Panthers. She managed to escape, and I'm trying to get her across the border and to the hospital."

"Do the police know about this?"

"They know she was kidnapped, but I haven't let them know that she's escaped. I thought it would be safer to get her across the border first."

The officer frowned, and then nodded. "There's been some trouble with the Mexican police being on the payrolls of several different drug cartels, so I can understand your concern. How about we move inside? We'll check out your story and see what the police have to say."

"Sounds good." Anything to get Jenna out of the open.

A female officer finished frisking Jenna and stepped back, nodding with satisfaction. "She's clean."

Nikolai took Jenna's forearm, steering her toward the narrow border patrol station. "Are you okay?"

"Fine. I even think my vision is returning." She offered a brief smile, but her pallor and the tentative way she moved belied her words.

"Are you able to see light?" He slipped an arm around her waist, knowing that she needed the support whether she wanted to admit it or not.

"I think I'm seeing shadows moving. Or maybe it's just wishful thinking."

"There's nothing wrong with wishing."

"No, but wishes usually don't come true. If they did, I'd wish bigger than getting my vision back."

"Yeah?"

"I'd wish Magdalena were here with me." Her voice broke, and Nikolai tugged her closer to his side.

"It really is going to be okay, Jenna."

"For me, but that's not what I'm worried about."

It *was* what Nikolai was worried about. He didn't have time to say it.

One minute Jenna was walking and talking, the next she was slipping out of his grasp. He just managed to catch her, pulling her up into his arms and shouting for the border patrol officer to call for an ambulance. As he looked down into Jenna's colorless face, he could only pray that the ambulance would get there in time.

THREE

Gray and black. Shadows and light. Fuzzy images that didn't quite make sense. Jenna blinked, trying to bring the hospital room into focus. There was a clock on the wall, but she couldn't make out the time. That was just as well. She wasn't sure she wanted to know how many hours had passed since she'd arrived at the hospital, or how much time had passed since she'd last seen Magdalena.

Too much time. There's no way she's still alive.

The thought flitted through her mind and lodged there, the words repeating over and over again until Jenna wanted to scream.

Magdalena was *not* dead.

She was alive and waiting to be found.

Jenna refused to believe anything else.

Refused to, but the thought was still there, echoing through her mind, chasing her out of the bed she'd been brought to just a few minutes before.

She swayed, the IV needle in her arm pulling a little as she grabbed the bed railing to keep from falling. The throbbing agony in her head intensified as she crossed the room and pulled open a heavy curtain, letting in bright sunlight that seared its way into her skull.

She winced, pulling the curtains closed again, sweat beading her brow, her body shaking from the pain. It didn't matter, though. Nothing mattered except finding out what had happened to Magdalena. She wanted to pull out the IV, walk out the door and search for her friend, but she knew she wouldn't make it out of the hospital parking lot. She had no car. No other means of transportation. Even if she had, how far would she get with severely limited vision?

Jenna scowled as she paced back across the room, grabbed her clothes from a pile on a chair and pulled on her jeans. Her T-shirt wouldn't go on over the IV, so she tossed it back onto the chair. She'd never been one to give up easily, and she wouldn't give up now. There had to be a way to get back to Mexico.

But was going back the right thing to do?

God had brought her safely out of a dangerous situation. Should she throw herself back into it?

She didn't know, couldn't concentrate enough to figure it out.

I wouldn't mind a clue, Lord. Some hint as to what You want me to do. She prayed as she paced to the chair in the corner of the room. A small table stood beside it, and Jenna could see something lying on top of it. She reached out, felt soft leather. Her purse. It had to be. She opened it, checking for her passport and wallet. Neither were there. Nikolai must have brought the purse into her room and left it while she was down in radiology.

Nikolai who had found his way into a drug cartel's stronghold and freed her. He'd said he'd done so as a favor to her brother, and he'd said he would go back for Magdalena as soon as he got Jenna to safety. Had he? Jenna grabbed a blanket from the bed and tossed it around her shoulders, determined to find out. It seemed to take too much effort to open the door, and she swayed as she stepped out into the hall.

"Going somewhere?" The deep, gruff voice was so unexpected, Jenna jumped, whirling to face the speaker and regretting it immediately. Lights flashed in front of her eyes, the world spun and she was falling. Firm hands wrapped around her upper arms, supporting her until it settled back into place.

"Thanks." She took a step back, looking up into a rugged, handsome face. Nikolai's face? It had to be. The voice, the gentle strength of the hands—those were things she'd never forget.

"You can thank me by sitting down. I don't think a woman with a fractured skull should be walking around."

She didn't argue as she was urged down into a chair against the wall outside her room.

"Better?" Nikolai crouched in front of her, and she could just make out dark hair and striking features. High cheekbones. A strong jaw.

"Yes. Thanks."

"You're supposed to be in bed resting."

"And you're supposed to be on your way back to Mexico to find Magdalena." Even as she said it, she knew how ungrateful she sounded. He'd saved Jenna's life, and she had no right to ask him for more. "I'm sorry, that wasn't what I meant to say."

"No apology necessary. I said I would go, and I would have, but Border Patrol won't let me back into Mexico."

"Then, I'll go." She started to rise, but he put a hand on her arm, holding her in place.

"You know that won't work, Jenna."

"It might. I just need my passport. Do you have it?"

"Yes."

"Good. I'll get a nurse to take out this IV, and I'll be on my way." She struggled to her feet, and this time he didn't try to stop her.

"To do what? Border Patrol isn't any more likely to let you cross the border than it was me." His voice was gentle, and Jenna blinked back tears she'd been refusing for hours.

"If they won't, I'll find another way to get across."

"Do you really think I'm going to let you make an attempt at an illegal border crossing?"

"You did your job, Nikolai. You got me out of Mexico. What I do now is up to me."

"Not if you aren't thinking clearly."

"I'm thinking plenty clearly."

"Telling yourself that won't make it true and throwing yourself back into danger won't save your friend."

"I have to at least try." She stepped to the door, her stomach roiling, stars dancing in front of her eyes.

"You've got a fractured skull and you can't see…"

"My vision is coming back. The doctors said it should be completely normal in a few hours."

"Jen, you can barely walk."

"I'm fine!" But she wasn't. Not fine enough to take another step let alone attempt to walk across the border into Mexico.

Nikolai must have sensed her defeat. He slid an arm around her waist, supporting her as they walked back into the room.

She dropped onto the bed, blinking hard to bring Nikolai into sharper focus. "I just want her to be okay."

"I know." He pulled a chair over and sat across from her.

"If she's not—"

"You'll go on. That's how life is."

"You make it sound as if it's a done deal. Do you know something I don't?"

"All I know is that your friend is still missing. I called the Mexican police less than an hour ago, and they still haven't located her."

"But they're looking?"

"Of course."

"And?"

"They've searched the building where I found you, but it's empty. The Mexican Panthers cleared everything out before the police arrived."

"You've mentioned them before."

"Who?"

"The Mexican Panthers. I'd never heard of them before today."

"Consider yourself fortunate. They're one of the most notorious drug cartels in Mexico, and they don't believe in letting their enemies live."

"I don't understand what that has to do with me or Magdalena."

"Neither do the Mexican police or the DEA. It's what they're hoping to find out."

"What do you mean?"

"Exactly what I said. The Mexican Panthers are quick to murder enemies, but they're not known for taking out innocent people."

"You're not implying that Magdalena and I were involved in the drug trade, are you? Because if you are—"

"I'm not implying anything. I'm telling you what the police are probably thinking."

"Then, they're thinking wrong."

"Maybe. Or maybe there's information that you know nothing about. Something that might have led the Mexican Panthers to you and your friend."

"Like?"

"It's possible Magdalena—"

"No way." There was absolutely no way that Magdalena was involved in drug trafficking.

"Hear me out, Jenna." He leaned close, his dark eyes staring into hers. Were they brown? Dark blue? She couldn't tell, and she was tempted to move closer, look more deeply.

She leaned back instead, unsettled in a way she hadn't been in years.

She didn't like the feeling.

Didn't like it at all.

"Say what you need to say, Nikolai, but it won't change what I know about Magdalena."

"It's possible your friend wasn't the person you thought

her to be. She may have had secrets she couldn't share with you."

Magdalena *had* seemed tense in the weeks leading to the trip, but Jenna had chalked it up to stress. Was it possible something else had been weighing on her mind?

Jenna shook her head, denying her doubts as much as she was denying Nikolai's words. "Everyone has secrets, but Magdalena's weren't the kind that get people killed."

"Then perhaps Magdalena got in the way of a transaction between someone she knew and the drug cartel. Is it possible someone working at the clinic was trafficking in narcotics?"

"I don't know. There were fifteen people on our medical team, and Magdalena is the only one I knew." Jenna shook her head, wincing as pain shot through her skull. Her stomach heaved and she swallowed hard. No way did she plan to lose her lunch in front of Nikolai. She bent forward, trying to ease the nausea, wishing her thinking was less muddled. Maybe Nikolai was right and someone at the clinic *had* been involved in drug smuggling, but she couldn't think of who it might be. Couldn't even begin to imagine any of the volunteers stooping so low.

Nikolai touched her knee, his fingers warm through thick denim. "Why don't you lie down? I'll make some more phone calls. Perhaps the police have new information."

"I'm okay." She straightened, sweat beading her brow as her stomach heaved again.

"You're as pale as a ghost."

"So maybe I should have said that I *will* be okay." She stood, swaying as she took a step toward the window.

Her vision seemed to be clearing, the steroids the doctors were pumping into her doing their job. God was in control, and everything would work out okay. It was a mantra that she'd repeated to herself often during the two years she'd fought leukemia. Chemotherapy had sapped her strength, turned her into a person she didn't know, and she'd had to remind herself every day that she'd be herself again when it was over. When it finally was, when she'd thought she would celebrate with longtime boyfriend Ryan Mayer and had, instead, listened as he'd told her how much he cared about her and how sorry he was that he'd fallen in love with someone else, she'd reminded herself that she would be okay. Her hair would grow back, her body would be strong again, her heart would heal.

Yes, God *was* in control, and Jenna *would* be okay.

But would Magdalena?

Jenna wanted to believe that she would be. Wanted to have hope that Magdalena would be found alive and healthy and anxious to go back to her husband and son.

She wanted to, but hope was elusive, her hold on it tentative. She swallowed back tears and turned away from the window, nearly falling backward when she realized Nikolai was right behind her.

"Careful." He grabbed her hand, holding her steady as she regained her balance, the warmth of his touch seeping into her chilled flesh.

"Thanks." She pulled her hand away, her cheeks heating for reasons she refused to acknowledge.

"You look feverish. I'll call the nurse, and—"

"No!" She nearly shouted, her cheeks heating even more. "You've already done plenty, Nikolai. Actually, you've done *more* than plenty. You saved my life, and I won't ever forget it. I hope you know that."

"It sounds like you're getting ready to say goodbye." He offered a half smile that transformed him from handsome to drop-dead gorgeous, and Jenna's heart skipped a beat.

"It's time, isn't it? I'm safe in the hospital, and I'm sure you have a lot of other things you could be doing."

"I can't think of anything."

"You could go home."

"Now it sounds like you're kicking me out."

"I'm not, but I'm sure my brother will be here soon, and there's no need for you to wait for him to show up."

"I spoke to Kane after we arrived at the hospital. He'll be here in about an hour. I'll take off once he arrives—"

"You really don't have to—"

"I want to. Besides, my flight to Houston doesn't leave until tonight."

"Houston?"

"I live there."

"So does Magdalena."

"I know."

"What else do you know?"

"That she's a pediatrician who specializes in orthopedic surgery and that she's been running medical clinics in Mexico for several years. That she has a three-year-old son named Benjamin and a husband named John."

"You've been busy."

"I like to know the people I'm searching for."

"Searching for?" Surprised, Jenna stepped toward him, misjudging the distance and bumping into his chest. She blushed as he grabbed her arms, steadying her for what seemed like the hundredth time.

"You're not the only one who doesn't believe in leaving people behind. I haven't given up on going back across the border. I've got some friends in Houston who may be able to help me do it."

"Who—" She was interrupted by a sharp rap on the door, and Nikolai whirled toward the sound, his broad frame blocking Jenna's view.

She stepped sideways, her stomach dropping as she saw a suited man standing in the threshold of the door. He was bringing news. Jenna was sure of that, but her vision was still too impaired to read his facial expression.

"Jenna?"

"Yes?"

"I'm Agent Skip Bradley with the DEA." He pulled something from his pocket and held it out, but Jenna couldn't make out any details.

Nikolai moved toward the man, offering a hand. "I'm Nikolai Jansen."

"Good to meet you, Nikolai. I'd like to speak with Jenna in private. I'm sure you won't mind waiting out in the hall."

"Actually, I would."

"I'm going to have to insist."

"I'm sure you are, but I'm not going anywhere until Jenna's family arrives." Nikolai pressed a hand to Jenna's back, urging her to the chair.

She sat quickly, her head spinning from the movement. "Do you have news, Agent Bradley?"

"I'm afraid that's why I'm here."

Afraid?

That meant the news was bad. "You've found Magdalena?"

"The Mexican police found her body. She was shot execution-style and left on the side of the road about twenty miles from where you were being held."

Dead.

Magdalena was dead.

The words echoed through Jenna's mind, and she took a deep breath, trying to silence them. "You're sure it's her?"

"Her husband is flying to Mexico to identify the body, but we're confident it is."

"I see."

But she didn't.

How was it possible that Magdalena was dead? That a mission of mercy had turned into a death sentence?

Nikolai squeezed her shoulder, his hand resting there as Agent Bradley continued. "I'm really sorry to have to bring you this news, Jenna, but we're hoping that something you know can help us find your friend's killers."

"Magdalena was one of the kindest, most selfless people I've ever known. I can't think of any reason why someone would want to harm her."

"Would it surprise you to know we found thousands of dollars worth of cocaine hidden inside the lining of her suitcase and purse back at the hotel room you shared?"

"Nothing would surprise me at this point." She stood, pacing across the room, away from Agent Bradley's questions and Nikolai's gentle support.

"Did you know it was there?"

"Of course, I didn't. Neither did Magdalena."

"It seems unlikely that Magdalena didn't know what was hidden in her things," Bradley responded, a hint of impatience in his voice.

"I've told you what I know and what I believe. I'm not sure what else you want me to say."

"Who did she spend time with when she wasn't working at the clinic?"

"Me. A few of the other medical professionals who were on the mission trip with us."

"She didn't go on errands alone? Perhaps take a few late-night strolls?"

"We were only there a couple of days, and she never went anywhere alone during that time."

"How about phone calls?"

"What about them?" Jenna's temper rose, washing over her in a wave that drowned out fatigue and pain and sorrow.

"You sound upset."

"Of course, I'm upset. My best friend is dead. Murdered. And you're accusing her of being involved in drug trafficking."

"I'm not accusing. I'm questioning."

"I don't see the difference."

"We need answers, Jenna. I'm sure you understand that."

"I'm giving them to you, but I get the impression you'd rather me tell you a fantastic tale about late-night phone calls and strange disappearances than the truth."

"The truth is that your friend was executed by the Mexican Panthers. The truth is it wasn't just a random act."

"It had to be." Jenna bit back her temper, knowing it wouldn't help. Losing control never made things easier, and it certainly wouldn't convince Agent Bradley that she was telling the truth.

"Did you miss the part where I told you that Dr. Romero had thousands of dollars worth of illegal drugs in her suitcase and purse?"

"Someone else must have put that there. Magdalena was absolutely opposed to illegal drug use."

"Who would have done that? When?"

"I don't know. I just know that it wasn't hers."

"You *think* that it wasn't, but—"

"It's your job to find the truth, Agent Bradley, so perhaps you should go do that." Nikolai broke into the conversation, and Bradley stiffened.

"Part of finding the truth involves interviewing people who knew the deceased."

The deceased.

He said it as if Magdalena were a faceless, nameless body. Someone who had lived and died and whose life no longer had value.

"The *deceased* was a woman of integrity. The *deceased* had a son and a husband who loved her and hundreds of patients who respected and admired her. The deceased was a dear friend of mine, and if you think that I'm going to roll over and play dead while you accuse her of drug-related crimes, you've got another thing coming."

"All I'm asking you to do is think back over your time in Mexico. See if there's something that stood out as odd or out of character for Magdalena. Perhaps she was pressured into carrying those drugs. Perhaps someone on the team pulled her into something she didn't want to do."

"She wasn't like that. She couldn't be pressured into doing something illegal or immoral," Jenna said, but knew Agent Bradley wouldn't believe her. Did it even matter? They could argue all day and it wouldn't bring Magdalena back. That thought was a splash of ice water that cooled Jenna's temper, stole the energy that had pulsed through her. Her legs went weak, her body numb, and she wasn't sure how much longer she could stay on her feet.

"Is it possible that she—"

"I don't think I'm up to this, after all. Maybe we could finish the interview another time," Jenna cut him off, dropping onto the edge of the bed.

"It's imperative that we get as much information from you as soon as we can."

"She said that she was done." Nikolai spoke before Jenna could, stepping between her and the agent and bending down to look into her eyes. "Would you like me to call the nurse?"

"No. I just need to close my eyes for a while." What she really needed was to be alone with her thoughts so that she could wrap her mind around what Agent Bradley was saying, what he was accusing Magdalena of.

"I'm sure Agent Bradley understands that."

"I'll come back in a few hours. I'm sure you'll be feeling well enough to answer more questions by then." There seemed to be a threat behind the agent's words, and Jenna was still letting it sink in as the sound of footsteps and voices drifted in from the corridor.

"Ms. Dougherty?" A nurse stepped into the room. "You have another visitor."

A tall, masculine figure appeared behind her. "Hey, sis. Sorry it took me so long to get here."

"Kane?" She wanted to say more, but her voice caught.

"Who else?" He hurried across the room, his dark hair and familiar face so welcome, Jenna blinked back tears of relief.

"Magdalena is dead." She said it without thinking, the truth bursting out and into the air, hanging there.

"I know. I heard on my way here." He sat beside her, putting an arm around her shoulders.

"I should have tried harder to keep them from taking her."

"You did everything you could." He smoothed her hair just as he had when she was a kid and had run to him with a scraped knee or a bruised ego.

She didn't respond, just closed her eyes, fighting back tears, knowing that if she let them fall, she'd never stop crying.

"I'll come back in a few hours." Agent Bradley spoke quietly, and for the first time since he'd entered the room, he sounded compassionate rather than businesslike.

"I'll walk you out," Nikolai said, and Jenna forced her eyes open.

"Will you be coming back?"

"Do you need me to?"

It was an odd question, and despite the fact that Kane was sitting beside her, Jenna almost said yes. "I guess not."

"Then I'll leave for the airport. I've got some business to take care of in Houston."

But not the business he'd spoken of before. There would be no effort to cross the border, no desperate search for a missing woman. Magdalena had been found, and the truth of her death settled deep into Jenna's heart. A tear rolled down her cheek, and she brushed it away, closing her eyes again, and turning her face so that the men wouldn't see. Footsteps sounded on the tile floor, and someone leaned close. She could feel his warmth, smell the mint that seemed to hang on the air around Nikolai. A warm finger traced the path her tear had taken, but she didn't open her eyes. Couldn't. Not without letting everything she was feeling out.

"It will be okay, Jenna. You will grieve, and then you will go on. That's how life is." Nikolai echoed the words he'd spoken earlier, his voice seeping into Jenna's self-imposed darkness.

She knew she should respond, but what was there to say? Magdalena was dead. Words couldn't change that, so she kept silent, listening as Nikolai said goodbye to Kane and walked away.

FOUR

Hundreds of mourners picked their way across rain-soaked earth, following the pallbearers to a large tent covering the open grave. Black umbrella butted against black umbrella, the drip of rain and rustle of fabric mixing with hushed conversation and the slosh of feet on wet grass. Nikolai followed the crowd, his eyes on the vibrant blue umbrella near the head of the pack. It had been a week since he'd seen Jenna, but he had no trouble conjuring up an image of her face. He'd thought about her often in the days since he'd left her at the hospital.

Too often.

He'd wondered how she was doing. Worried that her vision hadn't returned the way it was supposed to. He'd found himself calling Kane to check in on a daily basis, had almost given in to temptation and gone to the airport the day Jenna and her family had flown in for the funeral. That annoyed him. He was, after all, a confirmed bachelor. A guy who enjoyed freedom from the trappings of family and relationships.

At least he had been.

Things had changed in the past year. He'd reconnected with the sister he'd thought had been lost to him forever. He'd accepted a job working for Information Unlimited. He'd found himself with family ties and career ties, a small apartment in Houston and a church family that prayed for him when he was on assignment.

And now he found himself attending the funeral of a woman he didn't know, offering support to someone he barely knew.

For sure he was changing, and he wasn't sure he liked it.

He skirted past a young couple carrying a crying toddler, bypassed several older couples and found a spot a dozen yards from the gravesite. Rain splashed onto his head and dripped down his face, but he didn't bother wiping it away.

Under the tent, the pastor began to speak, his deep voice carrying across the cemetery, the words meant to comfort. How, though, could one find comfort in death? Even knowledge of God and Heaven did not take away the sting of goodbyes said too early. Nikolai had said enough of them to know that.

Magdalena Romero had been shot in cold blood. The truth of that tainted the victorious message of everlasting life that the pastor offered. Had a woman so admired by so many been involved in drug trafficking? That seemed to be the angle the DEA was pursuing. Nikolai had heard the same from the Mexican police he'd spoken to.

Yet Jenna was convinced of her friend's innocence.

Either way, a young mother was gone, her son childless, her husband a widower.

The pastor finished speaking and family members placed pink and white roses on top of the casket. One by one, the mourners who'd braved the weather did the same. One by one, they said their goodbyes, shook the rain off their shoes and got back into their cars. A dark-haired man ushered a toddler away from the grave. The little boy splashed in a puddle near one of the limousines. Was he Magdalena's child? If so, he was much too young to understand the finality of his mother's death and burial.

It didn't take long for the gravesite to empty of all but a few mourners. The dark-haired man and the child were joined by an older couple, and the four climbed into the limousine. The driver slowly pulled away.

Jenna stood beneath the tent, her umbrella held loosely in

her hand. Kane and an older couple stood to her right. She said something, and the three walked toward a dark sedan parked nearby, leaving Jenna in front of the casket.

Alone, she seemed much smaller than Nikolai remembered. More fragile and less tough. In his memory, she'd been someone for whom losing would never be an option. Looking at her now, seeing her bowed shoulders and head, he had the impression of defeat rather than victory.

Grass and water sloshed under his feet as he crossed the space between them. The tent was nearly empty, the funeral home staff hovering a respectable distance away, waiting for the last mourner to leave. Hundreds of roses covered the gleaming mahogany casket, and the area surrounding the grave was littered with glistening petals. Nikolai lay his rose on top of the pile, saying a silent prayer for Magdalena's family.

"She would have loved this." Jenna spoke quietly, and Nikolai turned, his breath catching as he looked into her eyes. He'd been wrong to think she was vulnerable, to believe that she was defeated. There was fire in her pale blue eyes, and a need for revenge that Nikolai understood only too well.

"You're Nikolai, right?" She smiled and took a step toward him, the scent of vanilla hanging in the air as she offered her hand.

"That's right." He clasped hands with her, feeling the strength of her fingers and the calloused ridges on her palms.

"I thought so, but my vision wasn't that great when we last saw each other, and I wasn't sure."

"I wondered if you'd recognize me."

"I almost didn't. I wasn't expecting to see you again."

"I wanted to pay my respects, and I wanted to see how you were doing."

"Thank you. For both things." She stepped past him, the scent of vanilla stronger as she placed her hand on the lid of the coffin. "She was much too young to die."

"Isn't everyone?"

She glanced over her shoulder, offering a sad smile. "I suppose so, but Magdalena really was young. Just thirty. With a young son who needed her." She shook her head, let her hand fall away from the casket. "It shouldn't have happened. I want to know why it did."

"Your brother told me that when we spoke last."

"And that's why you're really here? To make sure I don't go running off to Mexico in some mad quest for revenge?"

"I already told you why I'm here."

"And it has nothing to do with the fact that my brother needs to get back to Washington and doesn't want to leave me here for a few days?"

"He mentioned that, but it's not my reason for coming."

"No? So Kane never asked you to play bodyguard when he returns to Spokane?"

"Not in so many words."

"I knew it. I'm going to have to have a talk with that brother of mine." She would have walked away, but Nikolai put a hand on her arm, holding her in place. Despite the fire in her eyes and the calluses on her hands, she was very thin, her bone structure fine. He loosened his grip, not wanting to bruise her.

"Your brother simply asked me to check in on you a few times while you were in Houston. Since I live just a few miles from the hotel, it wasn't an unreasonable request."

"You don't need to check in on me at all, Nikolai. I'm perfectly capable of taking care of myself."

"That's what I told your brother."

"Yet you're still here."

"Would you rather I not have come?"

She frowned, smoothing a hand over her hair, her thick bangs parting to reveal the fading bruise on her forehead. "I'm sorry. I don't know what's wrong with me lately. Too many people asking too many questions that don't make sense, I guess. But, then, none of this makes sense." She gestured to the casket. "I still can't believe she's gone."

"How are her husband and son holding up?"

"John is…stoic. There's been a lot of media attention surrounding the case, and I think he's trying to keep his emotions in check. Little Benjamin keeps asking when his mother is coming home. I don't think he can wrap his mind around the word *never*. He's too young to understand and too young to retain many memories of his mother."

"He'll have you and his father and his family to remind him."

"Yes. That's true." She turned back to the casket, bowing her head, perhaps praying as Nikolai had done. Did she wonder, as he often did, how God could allow good people to die so brutally? Or did she simply accept that the world was a sinful and fallen place and that tragedy was not limited to those who truly seemed deserving of it?

The wind gusted, blowing rain under the tent and scattering rose pedals across the slick green grass. Jenna shivered. "I guess this is it, then. Goodbye, dear friend." She kissed her fingers, set them on the casket one last time and turned away.

Nikolai fell into step beside her as she walked away, not speaking, knowing there was nothing he could say that would ease Jenna's grief.

The silence lasted until they reached the black sedan and the door opened, Kane stepping out into the rain. "Umbrellas are more useful when they're open, Jen. You'd better get in the car where it's dry," he said, nodding a greeting at Nikolai.

"A little rain never hurt anyone," she responded, not bothering to do as he'd asked. "Will you be coming to the reception, Nikolai?"

"I understood it was only for close friends and family."

"And their guests. There's no reason why you can't be one of mine."

"It might be best if I leave the family to their privacy."

"John is expecting 150 people. I don't think privacy is something he's worried about. Besides, I had a proposition I'd like to discuss with you."

"A proposition?"

"A job."

"What are you talking about, Jenna?" Kane sounded exasperated, and Jenna patted him on the arm.

"Nothing worrisome. I just needed some help doing some research. You said Nikolai does freelance work for you, and I thought he might like an extra job."

"Does this have something to do with Magdalena?"

"What if it does?" She met her brother's eyes, the fire back in her gaze.

"The men who killed your friend are dangerous, Jenna. I don't want you going after them. Leave that to the police."

"So far, the police haven't done squat. Will you come to the reception, Nikolai?"

The look Kane sent his way told Nikolai exactly what his answer should be, but he'd never been one to conform to others' expectations. Obviously, Jenna had a plan for finding her friend's killer. Obviously, she was going to keep searching until she found someone to help her. Nikolai wasn't sure he'd be the person to do that, but there was nothing wrong with hearing her out.

"Sure."

"Good. You can follow us over." Jenna's smile was brilliant, and Nikolai found himself smiling in return as she slid into the car and turned to speak to one of the occupants.

"You're not seriously considering helping my sister," Kane asked quietly, and Nikolai's smile fell away.

"It depends on what she needs and what she's willing to pay."

"That's rather mercenary, even for you."

"It is what it is." Nikolai shrugged, not at all offended by Kane's assessment. If he chose to help Jenna, he'd probably do it free of charge. But that was his business and his decision, not something he planned to discuss with Kane.

"She's been through a lot in the past few years, Nikolai. Don't make things worse by stringing her along, promising her something you can't deliver."

"If I promise her something, I'll deliver."

Kane frowned, but didn't push the conversation any further. He'd been the one, after all, who'd called Nikolai when he couldn't reach Jenna by phone during her trip to Mexico. He'd been the one to call him and ask him to check on Jenna during her stay in Houston.

"Are you two done? We need to head over to the reception," Jenna called out from the car, and Kane nodded, shooting Nikolai a hard look as he got in and closed the door.

Nikolai ignored it. He wanted to know Jenna's plan. Only if he knew it could he be sure that she wasn't going to put herself right back in the path of danger. He jogged the few yards to his GTO and climbed in, following Kane to an upscale neighborhood on the edge of downtown Houston. Executive homes stood on large lots, their mature landscaping speaking of a well-established community. Dozens of cars lined the street, and Nikolai found a parking spot and waited as the Doughertys got out of their vehicle.

"I'm glad you came," Jenna called out as she walked toward him.

"It's not a problem."

"I'm sure my brother asked you not to."

"I did not," Kane said as he and an older couple joined Jenna. "I don't think you've met my parents, Nikolai. Lila and Richard Dougherty, this is Nikolai Jansen."

"Nice to meet you." Nikolai offered each a brief handshake.

"We can't begin to tell you how grateful we are for all you've done." Mrs. Dougherty pulled Nikolai into an unexpected hug, and Nikolai wasn't sure if he should pull back or let her have her way.

"Mom, give the poor man some room to breathe," Jenna said, tugging her mother away.

"Sorry, but I've been waiting nearly a week to thank you." Mrs. Dougherty patted his arm, and he smiled. Her eyes were the same pale blue as her daughter's, and looking at her gave him a glimpse into what Jenna would be like in thirty years.

"There's no need to thank me. I did what anyone would have, given the chance."

"You went above and beyond, and we won't forget it," Mr. Dougherty added, and Nikolai met his gaze, saw the worry there.

"Why don't you guys continue your lovefest inside?" Jenna broke in, her cheeks blazing.

"Good idea. Is that the house?" Nikolai gestured to a large Greek Revival that sat far back on a manicured yard.

"Yes."

"It's beautiful."

"It is," Jenna agreed, but she didn't sound like she meant it.

"You don't like it?" Nikolai walked up the driveway with her.

"It doesn't seem like Magdalena's style."

"What do you mean?"

"Big fancy house, big fancy lawn. She liked simpler things."

"Yet she lived here."

"John wanted something larger than the little condo they had downtown. This is the first time I've been to the house. The opulence surprised me." She reached out to ring the doorbell, but before she could, the door opened and a young man ushered them inside.

He took their coats and umbrellas, then disappeared, leaving them standing in a large foyer. Marble tiles gleamed in light from an ostentatious chandelier, and a wide curved staircase led to a second-story landing. Obviously, the doctor and her husband had been doing well financially.

"The reception is in the ballroom," Jenna said, leading the way through a long hallway.

"A ballroom? I thought ballrooms went out of style a century ago." Richard Dougherty spoke in a hushed voice as they made their way through wide double doors and into an expansive room.

"Apparently they're back in style," Kane replied, but Nikolai wasn't sure he agreed.

Maybe ballrooms were in vogue, but the cavernous room echoed with the sound of quiet conversation and clinking glassware, and Nikolai couldn't imagine that such a place would ever be in style. The waitstaff milled around the mourners, offering drinks and finger foods. Off to one side of the room, in a back corner where it was barely noticeable, a poster-sized photo stood on an easel.

"That's Magdalena. Would you like to see what she looked like?"

"Sure." He followed Jenna across the room and studied the photo of the dark-haired, dark-eyed woman. "She was lovely."

"As lovely on the inside as she was on the outside." A tall dark-haired man moved toward them, his brown eyes meeting Nikolai's briefly before he turned his attention to Jenna. "I'm glad you made it, Jen. I was worried this all might be too much for you so soon after..." His voice trailed off and he shook his head.

"You know I wouldn't be anywhere else, John."

John? As in John Romero, Magdalena's husband?

Before Nikolai could ask, the other man pulled Jenna in for a hug, keeping his arm around her waist as he met Nikolai's eyes again. "You must be Nikolai. I was hoping Jenna would ask you to come. I know that if my wife had survived, she would have wanted to thank you for saving her best friend's life."

"I'm sorry that I wasn't able to save her as well."

"I am, too, but I know that you did all you could." John offered a sad smile that didn't sit well with Nikolai. Something about the guy's response seemed rehearsed. As if he'd stood in front of a mirror and practiced just the right smile and just the right words.

Then again, his family had been in the spotlight since Magdalena's death. Some people were jumping to Magdalena's defense. Others were whispering about the possibility of drug addiction and illegal drug trafficking. Perhaps John merely wanted to avoid more undue attention and was hiding his true emotions because of that.

"How is little Benjamin doing?" Jenna's mother asked, and John offered a more relaxed smile.

"As well as can be expected. He's down in the playroom with some of his buddies. My mother and the nanny are watching them."

"I think I'll go down and see him." Jenna stepped away from John's arm, and Nikolai wondered if the embrace had made her uncomfortable. Did she know John well? Or were they simply two people brought together through their mutual love for Magdalena?

"Would the rest of you like a tour of the house? It was Magdalena's pride and joy. Showing it off makes me feel a little closer to her."

The Doughertys were quick to accept the offer, though Nikolai was sure he saw tension in Kane's shoulders as he walked away. Maybe he, too, sensed something phony about Magdalena's husband.

And maybe Nikolai was looking for trouble where there wasn't any.

He didn't join the group following Romero. Instead, he followed Jenna back through the large ballroom and into the corridor. He expected her to find the basement door and retreat to the playroom, but she veered to the left, walking into a large dining room. French doors opened onto a covered patio, and she pushed them open, walking out into the gray day.

She probably wanted to be alone, and Nikolai probably should have respected that. But there'd been something about the look in her eyes when Romero talked about his wife, something about the tension in her face that begged questions.

He crossed the room, walked out onto the patio. Rain pattered against the roof and dripped from the eaves, the sound quiet and soothing. "Did you come out to get away from the crowd or from Magdalena's husband?"

"Both," Jenna responded, not turning to look at him.

"You don't like him?" He walked up beside her, the wind splattering rain across the porch.

"Magdalena loved him."

"That wasn't my question."

"I've never thought my opinion of John mattered much. He was Magdalena's husband. He supported her dreams and her humanitarian missions. He's a good father to their son." She shrugged.

"But you've never liked him."

"I've never *not* liked him. It's just that aside from Magdalena, we had nothing in common. Now that she's gone, we have nothing to say to each other."

"Has he asked about your time in Mexico?"

"Once, but the details were too difficult for him to hear. Magdalena and Benjamin are his life, and he couldn't stand to think of Magdalena terrified and hurt." She shuddered, and Nikolai put a hand on her shoulder.

"I'm sorry for all you've been through, Jenna. I know how difficult it is to lose someone you love."

"Then you'll understand why I need your help."

"I understand that you want your friend's killer to go to jail, but you have to understand that the likelihood of that happening is slim to none."

"Did you think that's what I was going to ask you to do? Go after her killer?" She turned and they were inches apart, her hair dark with rain, her skin dewy. Long lashes brushed her cheeks as she blinked, and Nikolai found himself being pulled into her gaze, losing himself in the pale blue of her eyes.

"Is there something else that you need?"

"Magdalena was a woman of faith. She was committed to God, to her family and to humanity in that order. She never, ever would have done anything that would hurt another person. *Ever.* Now people are talking about her as if all the things she did while she was alive mean nothing."

"The circumstances of her death were unusual."

"That doesn't mean she was guilty of a crime."

"What is it that you want me to do, Jenna?"

"I want you to prove that Magdalena had nothing to do with the Mexican Panthers."

"That's a tall order."

"You seem like the kind of person who would be up for the challenge."

Nikolai could have said no. He'd said it before to other people in other situations. As sorry as he felt for Magdalena's family, he could have walked away, let things play out however they would. It was the responsibility of the Mexican police and the DEA to uncover the truth about why Magdalena had been executed.

He *could* have said no, but he'd always liked a challenge, and he'd always had a passion for the truth. And he found he couldn't look in Jenna's eyes, couldn't see the sorrow there and deny her request.

"I can't promise you anything."

"I don't need promises."

"Then I guess I'm your man," he said, before he could think better of it.

"Thanks." Jenna smiled, shivering again as the wind blew more rain under the porch.

"Thank me after I've done the job. Come on. We'd better go in before you freeze." He took her hand, started to lead her back to the door. A sharp crack split the air, and Nikolai dove for cover, grabbing Jenna by the waist and pulling her down, covering her body with his as another crack followed the first. Dirt and grass flew into his face, water and mud splashing into his eyes. He blinked it away, scanning the area beyond the porch. Trees lined the back edge of the property, and he was sure he saw someone there.

"What's going on? Is everything okay?" Someone called out from the house, and the figure in the trees moved away.

"You okay?" Nikolai looked down into Jenna's face.

"I will be once I can breathe again."

"Sorry." He stood, searching the tree line again, tracking the figure. "Go in the house, okay?"

"What—"

"Have someone call the police. I'll be back in a few minutes."

"Nik—"

He didn't wait to hear what Jenna said. The shooter had disappeared, and if Nikolai planned to catch him, the time for doing so was now.

And he *did* plan to catch him.

Jenna had escaped death in Mexico, but it seemed that it was hunting her again. Why?

It was a question only the gunman could answer, and Nikolai had every intention of making sure he did.

FIVE

Jenna pushed herself to her feet, her legs trembling so much that she wasn't sure she'd stay upright. Her palms were scratched and bleeding, and her head had renewed the pounding that seemed almost constant since she'd been injured in Mexico.

But things could be worse.

A lot worse.

She could be dead.

She shivered, the concerned voices of people inside the house barely registering as she tracked Nikolai's progress. He'd reached the tree line and slipped into the shadowy cover it provided. She wanted to follow him, but her legs weren't cooperating, and she stood frozen in place, staring at the trees and praying.

"What's going on? Jen?" Kane appeared at her side, his eyes filled with concern.

"I don't know. I think someone was shooting at us." Her voice was trembling, and that irritated Jenna. She didn't want to be scared, didn't want to feel weak and helpless.

"Can someone call the police?" Kane called out as he urged Jenna into the house. "Did Nikolai go after the guy?"

"Yes."

"I'll see if I can give him a hand."

"What's going on? Someone said they heard gunshots." John stepped into the room, pushing through the crowd that had formed, his hair mussed, his face pale. Jenna's mother and father were right behind him, and Jenna did her best to look less shaken than she felt. She'd given them too much to worry about in the past few years.

"Someone took a potshot at Jenna and her friend," Kane explained.

"I can't believe this." John smoothed his hair, frowning as his gaze dropped to Jenna's hands. "You're hurt."

"Just a few scrapes. I'll be fine."

"Why would someone do this?" Jenna's mother hurried to her side.

"We'll let the police figure that out." John pulled a cell phone from his pocket and dialed quickly.

"I'm going to help Nikolai search for the gunman." Kane disappeared outside, Jenna's father following him.

"If everyone else will go back to the ballroom, that would be great. I'm sure Jenna needs a few minutes to compose herself." John gestured to the door, and the crowd dispersed, excited whispers drifting from the hallway as they left.

"I just can't believe this happened the day of Magdalena's funeral. Haven't they already done enough?" John paced across the room and lifted a decanter from a shelf. "Would either of you care for a drink?"

"No. Thanks. Hasn't *who* already done enough?" And since when did John drink? In all the years Jenna had known him, she'd never seen him with anything more than an occasional glass of wine. Seeing hard liquor sitting in the dining room made her wonder if he'd changed in other ways as well.

"Who do you think? The Mexican Panthers. They stole my wife's life, and now they want to steal her reputation, ruin her in the world's eyes. I won't have it." He poured amber liquid into a shot glass and drank it quickly.

"I don't understand, John. How does trying to kill me accomplish that goal?"

"Trying to kill you? Do you really think they'd have missed

if that's what they were up to?" He poured another shot, took a sip.

"I don't know, but I don't think that drinking yourself into a stupor will do anything for Magdalena's reputation or for yours." Jenna spoke more sharply than she intended, and her mother gave a subtle shake of her head. Unlike Jenna, Lila had an easygoing and laid-back personality. She rarely lost her temper, and when she did, it was for good reason. Compassionate and empathetic, she had a nonjudgmental attitude, and Jenna knew she could learn a lot from her mother's example.

So far, she hadn't. Jenna was more the "tell it like it is" type. The kind who tended to speak first and think later. And no matter what the circumstances and hardship, she couldn't silently watch a grown man drown his sorrows when he had a young son to care for.

John stiffened, frowning down into the amber liquid before swigging the remainder of the drink. "Two drinks isn't exactly drowning my sorrows, Jenna. And after the week I've had, I don't think anyone could fault me if I *did* try to drown them."

"My point is that drinking won't change anything."

"You sound just like my poor wife. She was always nagging people to do things differently. Face your problems rather than hide them—that was her motto."

"That was one of the things I admired most about her." Jenna responded, surprised by John's words. Had he resented Magdalena? They'd seemed like such a strong couple, completely supportive of each other.

"Yeah. Me, too, but it makes her death even more shocking, don't you think?"

"I'm not sure I know what you mean."

"She was always trying to solve everyone else's problems, always rooting for the underdog and pushing for people to rise above their circumstances, and all along she had her own problems. Things she wouldn't face and never shared. If she had…" His voice broke, and Jenna stepped forward, put a hand on his arm.

"What are you talking about, John? What problems?"

"I didn't want to tell you this, Jen. I didn't want to ruin your memories of her."

"What?"

"Several DEA agents were here yesterday. They brought in dogs to search for drugs. They found…a lot. Magdalena had a hidden stash taped to the underside of her dresser drawer. She had more up in the attic. I don't know if she planned to sell them or use them. I just don't know." He dropped into a chair, rested his head in his hands, everything about him defeated.

"Maybe—"

"What? Maybe someone else put them there? Maybe our housekeeper or one of the workmen who did renovations when we bought the house? Don't you think I thought of that? Don't you think I told the DEA the same thing?"

"There's no way Magdalena was using illegal drugs. I would have known."

"Did you know she took methamphetamines during her last year of medical school?"

"What?! No!" Magdalena and drugs would never have gone together.

"She did. She—" Voices carried in from the still open French doors, cutting off John's words.

"The men are back. Thank goodness. I've been worried sick," Jenna's mother said, hurrying to the doors, embracing her husband as he walked into the study. "Did you see anyone?"

"Unfortunately, no. Are you okay, Jenna?"

"Yes." Only she wasn't. Not at all. Magdalena taking drugs during medical school didn't fit into the image she'd had of her friend. No matter how much she twisted and turned the information, it just didn't seem like something the woman Jenna had known would do.

"You don't look fine." Kane lifted her hands and studied the shallow scratches.

"You worry too much." She pulled her hands away, offering a smile that she didn't feel.

"And you don't worry enough. You didn't hit your head when you fell, did you? The doctor said—"

"I know what the doctor said, and I didn't hit my head." But she did have a headache, a pounding, splitting, horrible headache that she knew from experience wouldn't go away without heavy-duty painkillers and several hours of deep sleep. She couldn't afford either of those things. Not when she still had so many questions that needed answers.

"We did hit the ground pretty hard." Rain dripped from Nikolai's hair, sliding down his cheek as he approached. Handsome and compelling, he was a hero come to life. What woman wouldn't feel weak-kneed looking into his eyes?

"I hope I didn't hurt you," he said, his dark gaze scanning her face. Deep rich brown, that's what color his eyes were. She'd been wondering.

"Jenna?"

She pulled her thoughts up short, forcing herself to focus on the conversation rather than the man. Nikolai was, after all, nothing more than that, and she had more important things to wonder about than the color of his eyes. "I'm fine."

"You don't look fine." He lifted her hand, frowning as he saw the scrapes on her palm.

"A few bumps and bruises are nothing compared to a bullet. I really *am* fine."

Jenna took a few quick steps forward to prove her point, sharp pain shooting through her head at the movement. She swayed, reaching out to steady herself, her hand landing on something firm and hard.

She grabbed on, realizing a moment too late exactly what she was clutching. Biceps. *Nikolai's* biceps.

"Sorry." She released her hold, her cheeks heating as she met his eyes.

"No need to be."

"Sounds like the police are here," John said, rushing to the dining room door and gesturing to someone. "We're in here, Officers."

Seconds later, two officers appeared in the doorway.

"I'm Sergeant Lawrence and this is my partner Officer Daniels. We got reports of a shooting here," the shorter of the two said, frowning.

"That's right," John said. "Someone took a shot at one of my guests. I just buried my wife, and now I've got to deal with this." He nearly shook with indignation, and Jenna couldn't help thinking that he was overdoing the part of shocked host. The fact was, someone could have been killed. Indignation was the least of the things any of them should be feeling.

"Do you know who the target was?"

"I may have been." Jenna spoke up, not comfortable with the direction of her thoughts. Grief did different things to different people. Perhaps the only way John could deal with his grief was to focus on minute details and perceived injustices.

"You have reason to believe someone wants you dead?" Officer Daniels raised an eyebrow and pulled a notebook from his pocket.

"I was involved in some trouble in Mexico."

"Trouble?"

"The same Mexican drug cartel that murdered my wife tried to kill Jenna. She was fortunate to survive."

"And you think they may have followed you from Mexico?" the officer asked, his gaze on Jenna.

"I don't know." Until a few minutes ago, it hadn't occurred to Jenna that she might still be in danger. Not while she was in the hospital. Not when she'd flown to Houston and checked into the hotel with her family.

"The DEA is involved in the case. You can contact the agent in charge. I'm sure he'll be happy to fill you in on the details." John rattled off the name and phone number of the agent, and the officer scribbled it in his notebook, then looked up, cocking his head to the side.

"Your wife was Magdalena Romero?"

John stiffened, but nodded. "That's right."

"I've been following the news about her. I'm sorry for your loss."

"Me, too."

"Your wife was a good woman. She treated my son's clubfoot last year. Didn't charge a dime."

"That sounds like Magdalena."

"Does the DEA have any leads?"

"None." John didn't mention the drugs that had been found on the premises.

Would Jenna have if she were the one being questioned?

She didn't know. She only knew that Magdalena deserved to be remembered for the good she'd done. Not for her supposed crimes.

"Where were you when the shots were fired, Miss?" The sergeant walked to Jenna's side, his gaze jumping from Kane to Nikolai before finally settling on her face.

"On the patio."

"Did you see the shooter?"

"No."

"He was about five-foot-ten. 150 pounds." Nikolai seemed sure of the information, and Jenna met his eyes.

"You saw him?"

"Not enough details to identify him, but enough to give his height and build."

"And you are?" Sergeant Lawrence asked.

"Nikolai Jansen. I'm a friend of Jenna's."

"I see." The sergeant jotted something on a small pad of paper. "And you were with her at the time the shot was fired?"

"Shots. He fired twice. The first bullet hit a support beam. The second one hit the ground about half an inch from the edge of the porch."

"It seems like you had a good view of what was happening."

"Not until after the first bullet hit. I tried to get a visual on the shooter after that."

"Most people would have been more concerned about taking cover." There seemed to be a question hidden in the statement.

"I did that, too."

"You've had crisis training?" This time the question was overt, and Nikolai shook his head.

"Combat training. I saw action in Iraq and in Afghanistan."

"Yeah? I served four years myself. You an Army guy?"

"Marines."

"I'm Army, but the way I see it, military is military. Service to country is service to country."

"I couldn't agree more."

"So, you say you caught a glimpse of the shooter?"

"Not much of one. We went after the guy, but by the time we hit the tree line, he was gone."

"Why don't you take me out and show me which direction he headed. Daniels, you want to go see if there's evidence to collect on the porch? Mr. Romero, can you keep the guests here until we have a chance to question them?"

"Sure. I'll go let everyone know they'll need to stay for a while. Jenna, you want to come and help me explain?"

"Jenna looks a little shaken. How about I come and give you a hand." Jenna's mother patted Jenna's arm. "Go ahead and sit down, Jen. Once the police are done, we'll go back to the hotel and you can get some rest."

It sounded like a good plan. Maybe even a great one. Closing her eyes for a while, trying to forget that Magdalena was dead and that she had nearly been killed twice—those were things Jenna would love to do. But closing her eyes wouldn't solve any problems. It wouldn't bring Magdalena back or save Jenna from more trouble. All it would do was waste time better spent trying to find out the real reason for all that had happened.

Instead of sitting, Jenna followed the men out onto the porch. Rain still fell, splattering onto the soaked ground, the hushed thrum of it echoing through Jenna's pounding head. She felt sick. Whether it was from grief or fear or pain, she didn't know.

"The first bullet hit here," Nikolai said, pointing to splintered wood on one of the porch's support posts. Jenna had been standing just inches away from it when the bullet hit.

"And the second?"

"Right at the edge of the porch." Nikolai gestured to the spot, then stepped out from under the portico. "The shooter was right at the tree line after the first shot. He ducked into the trees after the second."

"Think you can take me to the spot? Maybe he left behind some forensic evidence. It's doubtful in this rain, but we'll take a look."

"Sure." Nikolai started toward the trees, Jenna's father and brother following, Sergeant Lawrence walking beside them.

Jenna wanted to follow, but her body refused to cooperate, and she stood where she was, staring at the hole in the wooden beam. She'd been close to death and hadn't even known it. If the gunman had better aim, or if it hadn't been raining, or if she'd moved a little to the right...

"Jenna?" Nikolai appeared in front of her, his tan face creased with worry.

"I'm all right."

"Not now, but you will be. Come on. Let's go back inside." He put his arm around her waist, and she allowed herself to be led back into the dining room.

"I thought you were helping Sergeant Lawrence."

"I showed him where I saw the guy. Your brother and father are taking him along the path we took through the trees."

"And you're here with me."

"You looked like you could use a friend."

"I could use some answers."

"I told you I'd help you find them."

"It doesn't make sense, Nikolai."

"Death never does."

"It's not just that." She hesitated, everything John had told her filling her mind.

"Then what is it?"

"John told me some things that just don't gel with what I know about Magdalena."

"Like?"

She told him, the words rushing out and tripping over each other, almost too surreal to repeat. When she finished he was silent, his expression unreadable.

"I don't believe it, Nikolai. I will never believe that Magdalena had a drug problem."

"How about her husband? Does he believe it?"

"He's on the fence."

"That's telling."

"How so?"

"Either he knows more than he's saying, or their relationship wasn't strong enough and he didn't know his wife well enough to stand by her in death. How long were they married?"

"Seven years."

"That's a good amount of time."

"They met in college and married while Magdalena was in medical school."

"And they've always lived in Texas?"

"Yes. Magdalena went to medical school here, and she fell in love with the area. After she and John married, they bought a condo near the hospital where she was doing her residency."

"And lived there until they moved to this place?"

"Yes." The move had surprised Jenna. The house had surprised her even more.

"As I said before, it's quite a place."

"It makes a statement, anyway."

"And you said it isn't the kind of statement Magdalena usually liked to make?"

"She didn't like to flaunt her wealth, if that's what you're asking."

"But she did have it, right? A place like this is expensive, and I don't imagine that a doctor who gave so much of her time to charity would have a ton of cash lying around."

"She wasn't trafficking drugs to finance her lifestyle. Her parents were both doctors. They left her a substantial trust fund when they died. And John is a defense attorney; he makes good money." Disgusted, Jenna stood and paced across the room, her head throbbing more with every step.

"You asked for my help, Jenna. I can't help if I don't ask questions."

Of course he couldn't, and Jenna didn't expect him to. She planned to tell him that, but as she turned to face him, the room tilted, the pain in her head exploding until all she could hear was her own heartbeat.

She swayed, reaching out, feeling Nikolai's hand anchoring her in place as the world spun around her.

"I think I need to sit down." She tried to speak, but the words were no more than a whisper, and she wasn't sure Nikolai heard.

Strong arms wrapped around her, holding her up as she slipped further into darkness.

Was she going to pass out?

No way.

Even at her sickest, even when chemo had stolen her strength, she'd never passed out. She wasn't going to do it now.

"Jen? What's going on?"

She heard Kane's voice, heard her father call her name through the thick darkness that was closing in.

And then she heard nothing at all.

SIX

Nikolai flipped through a six-month-old photography magazine, doing his best to ignore the antiseptic scent that filled the waiting room. After spending three months in a VA hospital, he'd sworn to stay far away from anything that even resembled a treatment facility. Yet here he was, exactly where he didn't want to be, sitting on a plastic seat, thumbing through an old magazine and praying that Jenna was all right.

The waiting room door opened, and Kane walked in, a cup of coffee in each hand. "Here you go."

"Thanks. Did you track down your sister and parents?"

"The nurse said they're down in radiology."

"Are they checking for brain injuries?" Nikolai hadn't seen Jenna hit her head, but that didn't mean it hadn't happened. He'd tackled her without much thought for anything except keeping her out of the line of fire.

"No." Kane's response was short, his face drawn with worry and fatigue. Aside from Jenna's injuries and troubles, Kane had a young son at home who needed him and a wife who was expecting a baby any day. The stress was starting to show.

"Then what?"

"They ran blood tests when she came in, and her counts are off."

"Which means?"

"I don't know. I'm not sure I want to speculate, either."

Kane dropped down into the chair beside Nikolai and took a sip of coffee.

"But you are speculating, so why not put it out there. Say what you're worried about."

"Jenna was diagnosed with leukemia four years ago. She's been cancer-free for two years."

"And you're worried that the cancer has returned?"

"I think that's what the doctors are worried about."

"Perhaps she's simply worn out. She's been through a lot. The body is more susceptible to illness when a person is under stress."

"Jenna's immunity is low anyway. She hasn't been the same since the chemo."

"I'm sure she wouldn't want to hear you say that."

"And if she did hear me, she'd deny it. She's always been independent and unwilling to show any weakness. I wouldn't put it past her to keep things from the family so that she wouldn't worry us."

"Like what?"

"Like a relapse."

"The way I see it, you can sit here and worry or you can find your parents and get more information. How about we go to radiology and see if they're there?" Nikolai stood, dropping the magazine back into the rack where he'd found it.

"It seems to me, I'm not the only one worried about Jenna."

"I don't think I've made any secret of the fact that I'm concerned."

"Concerned because you saved her life and want to make sure she stays alive or concerned because you've got a deeper interest in her?" Kane asked as they walked out of the waiting room.

"Is there a reason why you're asking? Other than idle curiosity, I mean."

"She's my sister. I don't want her hurt."

"She's already been hurt many times. You can't keep it from happening again."

"No, but I can warn you that I'd take a dim view of anyone toying with my sister's affections."

"That's an old-fashioned thing to say, Dougherty."

"I'm an old-fashioned guy."

He was also a brother with a younger sister he worried about. That, at least, was something Nikolai could identify with. "I have no intention of toying with anything."

"I'm glad to hear that. Come on. It looks like radiology is this way." They turned down a long corridor, walked through double doors and nearly bumped into Jenna's parents.

"Kane. Nikolai. Glad we ran into you. Jenna is on the way back up to her room." Jenna's father looked worn, his eyes shadowed.

"How is she?" Kane asked the question Nikolai wanted to and frowned as Richard shook his head.

"We won't know until the doctor finishes reviewing the CAT scan results."

"How long will that be?"

"An hour or so."

"That's an hour too long."

"I'm sure your sister feels the same way. We promised her a hamburger and a milk shake while she waits. How about we all go to the cafeteria and see if they have anything resembling that?"

"One of us should be up there with her." Kane spoke up, and Nikolai knew that any of the Doughertys would be happy to sit by Jenna's side. Whether or not she wanted them there was another story. The last thing Nikolai had wanted when he'd been confined to a hospital bed was sympathetic family sitting beside him watching with sad-eyed concern.

"Why don't I go up?" he asked, and all three family members turned their attention his way.

"I think Jenna would be more comfortable with one of us there." Kane responded before his parents could.

"Actually," his mother broke in, "Jenna insisted that we all get something to eat before we joined her. She's got a splitting headache, and she wants some time for the pain medicine to kick in."

"I'll wait outside the room, then, until she's feeling better." Because there was no way Nikolai was going to let her lie alone in a room waiting for whoever had shot at her to find her there.

"That's a wonderful idea, Nikolai. Would you like us to bring you something to eat or drink?" Once again, Mrs. Dougherty spoke up, offering a smile that reminded Nikolai of her daughter.

"No. Thanks."

"All right, then. Jenna is in room 306. We won't be long. Ready?" She took her husband's hand, hooked an arm around Kane's and steered them both down the hall.

Nikolai didn't waste time watching them walk away. The more he thought about Jenna alone in a hospital room, the less he liked the idea. Sure, there were people milling around the hospital, but that didn't mean Jenna was safe.

He hurried up to the third floor, bypassing a nurses' station, and stopped in front of Jenna's room. The door was closed, so he knocked, waited until he heard a muffled response and then walked in.

Jenna stood a few feet away, an IV dripping fluids into her arm as she buttoned a short-sleeved black shirt. She paused as he entered the room, her eyes wide with surprise. "I thought you were the nurse."

"I'm afraid not. I can find a nurse for you, though, if you need one."

"That's okay. I was just trying to figure out what happened to my socks."

"Socks?"

"My feet are freezing." She was still wearing the black slacks she'd worn to the funeral, and her bare toes peeked out from beneath the hem.

"If you were in bed, they wouldn't be."

"If I were in bed, I'd be thinking about…" Her voice trailed off, and she turned away, tugging the IV pole with her as she crossed the room and sat on the edge of the bed.

"What would you be thinking about?" he asked, even though he knew. She'd be thinking about the cancer coming back, about fighting the battle she'd won all over again. And maybe she'd be thinking that the next battle might be one she couldn't win.

"About how much my head hurts and about how much I don't want to spend the night in this room." Her skin was pale to the point of translucence, her freckles standing out in stark contrast. Deep red hair fell to her collar, the thick straight strands angling toward her jaw. Had she lost her hair during chemo? Her eyelashes and eyebrows? If so, had she worn a wig or had she painted art on her bald head and flaunted it for all the world to see? Nikolai imagined she'd done the latter. Could almost picture her, bald and beautiful, her head covered with colorful artwork.

"Will you be staying?"

"If the doctors and my family have their way. Unfortunately, I don't plan on falling in line and doing what everyone wants."

"If you did, I'd be disappointed."

She looked up and met his eyes, smiling for the first time since he'd entered the room. "Yeah?"

"You're a fighter. Why should you stop fighting now?"

"Funny, I was thinking the opposite before you walked in. I was thinking that maybe I should stop fighting and just let whatever is going to happen, happen."

"If you did that you wouldn't just disappoint me, you'd disappoint yourself."

"Maybe, or maybe I'd just be relieved." She smiled again, her lips colorless, her hand shaking as she brushed hair from her cheek.

"Your brother told me about the cancer, Jenna. Is that what

you're afraid of? Or are you afraid that the man who shot at you will try again?"

"Neither. And both. I know that whatever happens is in God's hands, and I know that I have nothing to fear, but I've just gotten my life back. I don't want to lose it again." She fiddled with the hem of her shirt, refusing to meet his eyes.

And Nikolai felt the same burning need to protect that he'd felt when he was a kid trying to keep his small and broken family together.

He reached out, tucking strands of silky hair behind Jenna's ear. "You won't lose it. I'll make sure of that."

She laughed, but there was no humor in the sound. "Do you really think it's up to you?"

"Inasmuch as I'm able, I'll keep you safe."

"I appreciate the thought, but it isn't necessary. As soon as the doctor clears me to leave, I'm getting on a plane and I'm going home. There's nothing more I can do here anyway. Magdalena is gone. Her husband seems content to let his parents help Benjamin heal."

"What about the Panthers?"

She shrugged. "I doubt they're so determined to kill me that they'll follow me all the way to Washington."

"They followed you here."

"Strange, don't you think? I was tied up and completely helpless, and they let me live. Now, they're trying to kill me. Why?" she asked as she rubbed her forehead.

"I've been wondering the same thing."

"And?"

"I don't have an answer, but I plan to get one."

"Let me know if you do, because I'm coming up blank." She closed her eyes, deep red lashes lying against pale skin.

"We can talk about this another time. Why don't you lie down and rest for a while?"

"Rest while my family and the doctors make plans about my treatment and discuss my diagnosis? I don't think so." But she didn't open her eyes.

Nikolai pulled a blanket from the end of the bed, and draped it over her, tucking it around her shoulders, his knuckles brushing her neck and cheek. Her skin was warm and incredibly smooth, and heat shot up his arm, settled deep in his belly.

He let his hand drop away and took a step back, stopping short when Jenna grabbed his wrist. "Are you leaving?"

"Do you want me to?"

"No. I need you to back me up when I tell everyone I'm planning to leave the hospital as soon as the nurse takes out this IV."

"Jen—"

"I hate hospitals, Nikolai. I spent the better part of two years in them, and I'm done. The smells, the sounds." She shuddered.

"I understand."

"Do you?"

"I've spent a fair amount of time in the hospital, too."

"Were you ill?"

"A roadside bomb nearly killed me in Iraq. I was in the hospital for three months being treated for burns on my legs. I nearly lost my right foot."

"I'm so sorry."

"Don't be. I survived, and I know how blessed that makes me. I also know how hospital smells can turn the gut. I'll back you up."

"Thanks."

"As long as the doctor doesn't think leaving is going to be detrimental to your health."

"Forget the thanks, then." She scowled, her eyes flashing with irritation.

"I told you I would do everything I could to keep you safe. If that means you have to stay in the hospital, that's what it means."

"And you really think I'm going to stay here just because

you, a few doctors and my family think I should?" She stood, fists settling on narrow hips.

"I think you're going to do whatever it takes to regain your strength so you can help me prove that Magdalena had nothing to do with the Mexican Panthers and drug trafficking."

"Don't try to be reasonable, Nikolai. I'm not in the mood."

The comment surprised a laugh out of him, and Jenna offered a weak smile in return. "Well, it's true."

"Then what are you in the mood for?"

"Answers, I guess. And my own bed in my own room in my own house with Dante warming my feet."

"Dante?" It hadn't occurred to Nikolai that there might be a man in Jenna's life. But, of course, there would be. She was that kind of woman. The kind who probably had a dozen suitors knocking at her door at any given moment.

"He's a scoundrel but I love him." She smiled, her expression more relaxed than it had been all day. Either Dante had provided her with many fond memories or the pain medicine she'd been given was kicking in.

"Have you known each other long?"

"Me and Dante?"

"Yes."

"I took him in about a year ago. Sometimes he disappears for a day or two, but I can't turn him away when he comes home."

The guy sounded like a loser, but it wasn't Nikolai's business. It *shouldn't* be his business, anyway. "What does Kane think of that?"

"Of Dante? I don't think he cares one way or another."

"That's surprising."

"Why? I've got my own place. The animals I keep there are none of my brother's concern."

Animals? "Dante is a dog?"

"A cat. Why? Did you think he was human?"

"He has a human name."

"Because he came scurrying out of my neighbor's fire pit about two seconds after Fred set a match to the wood and leaves in it."

"Dante's Inferno?"

"Exactly. Fred told me to let him run, but Dante was scrawny and homely, and I felt sorry for him."

"And now you own a cat."

"I don't own him. I just give him food and a place to stay." She smiled, glancing at her watch, some of her tension returning. "It's taking a long time for my family to come back."

"They're in the cafeteria."

"No, they're not. They've found the doctor and they're asking for complete disclosure. That way if it's bad news, they can come in and break it to me gently."

"Or they're waiting in a long cafeteria line."

"You forget, I've been through this before. Come on. We'd better find them." She grabbed his hand, her palm warm and dry against his as she walked to the door.

He could have protested. He might even have convinced her to wait for a while longer. But if he'd been in her position, he'd have gone searching, too, and he allowed himself to be pulled into the hall. Allowed himself to be pulled deeper into Jenna's life. At least that's what it felt like when she punched the elevator button and smiled up at him. That's what it felt like when they stepped off the elevator and saw her family talking to a man in a white lab coat.

"They don't look happy," Jenna whispered, stopping a few yards shy of the waiting group. "And I'm not sure I really want to know why."

"Whatever the doctor has to say, it'll be okay."

"You can't know that."

"No, but as you said, God is in control. I *do* know that, and it's enough. Come on."

"Okay." She took a deep breath, holding tight to his hand as she took the first tentative step forward.

SEVEN

It was bad news.

If it weren't, Jenna's father wouldn't have his game face on. If it weren't, her mother wouldn't look pale and shaken. If it weren't...

"Jenna, what are you doing down here?" her mother asked, and Jenna was sure there was a note of panic in her voice. Lila Dougherty never panicked.

So it *was* bad.

Worse, probably, than Jenna had been imagining.

"The same thing you are. I want my test results. Sitting around waiting for someone to come give me the news is driving me crazy."

"I was just on my way to your room when your parents found me. You really should have waited for us there." Dr. Shaw, a sixty-something man with a perpetual frown line between his brows, shot Jenna a look of disapproval.

"Perhaps if you'd come a little sooner, she would have." Nikolai's dry comment was met with another disapproving look.

"As I said, I was on my way up, but I saw Jenna's family and wanted to tell them that the police are in the waiting room. They'd like to speak with her."

Was that the bad news Jenna could see in her parents' faces? "That's fine."

"Actually, Jen, we already had a run-in with them, and it

might be best if we put off their questions for a while longer."
Kane frowned, his gaze falling to Jenna's hand. The hand
that was clutching Nikolai's. She dropped it quickly, her face
heating. What in the world was she doing? Obviously, the pain
medication was making her loopy.

"I don't mind talking to the police. The more questions I
answer the more likely it will be that they'll find the guy who
tried to shoot me."

"You'd think that would be the direction they'd be heading."
Kane muttered as he glanced up the hall.

"What do you mean?"

"How about we discuss this after Jenna returns to her
room?" Dr. Shaw broke in. "It's best if she rests as much as
possible."

His words sent Jenna's pulse racing, all her anxiety rearing
up again. "Why? What did you find?"

"That you haven't been taking care of yourself since your
release from the hospital. You're dehydrated, anemic and obviously exhausted. The best thing you can do for yourself is get
proper nutrition, plenty of fluids and a lot of rest."

"That's it?" Relief poured through her, and she felt light-
headed and dizzy with it.

"Aside from the healing fracture in your occipital bone,
the CAT scan was clean."

"So I can leave?"

"How about we discuss this in your room, Jen? I'd rather
not run into the police down here."

"I already told you that I'd answer their questions, Kane.
I've got nothing to hide."

"That's not what they're thinking, sweetheart." Jenna's
father rubbed the bridge of his nose, something he only did
when he was stressed out and worried.

"What exactly are they thinking, then?"

"That you may have been collaborating with Magdalena."

"Collaborating on what?" Frustrated, she tried to keep the

bite out of her tone, but knew she was doing a poor job of it. And that frustrated her even more.

"You know they think Magdalena was involved in drug trafficking, sis. Take another giant leap of logic and that'll take you exactly where they've gone."

"Let them go wherever they want. I've got nothing to hide."

"Neither did Magdalena." Nikolai spoke quietly, but his words echoed loudly in Jenna's mind. She'd never believe that Magdalena was involved in the drug trade, and she'd never have believed that the DEA would find drugs hidden in her bags and in her home. They had, though.

"They're trying to get a search warrant for your house, Jenna. You may as well know that now." Kane's voice was tight with frustration.

"I'd say that they won't find anything, but look what happened to Magdalena. They found plenty." *Would* they find something in Jenna's house if they searched it? The thought filled her with cold dread.

"It would be best if you all discuss this in Jenna's room. As I said, she needs to rest. We'll admit her for the night and release her in the morning once she's better hydrated." Dr. Shaw glanced at his watch, his impatience obvious.

"I'll rest better at home. Can you please send a nurse up to take out this IV?"

"I strongly recommend that you stay here for the night."

"It's a good idea, Jen, and it might keep the police from bothering you," Kane said falling into step beside her as she started walking back to the elevator. Nikolai flanked her on the other side, and Jenna had a quick glimpse of her future. Only rather than walking between Nikolai and Kane, she'd be walking between two police officers with handcuffs around her wrists.

"Do you have a friend you can call? Someone who can be in your house if the police do get a warrant?" Nikolai's practical question pulled her from her unhappy musings.

"My neighbor will be happy to supervise, but I'd rather he not have to. If I can get a ticket out of town tonight, I'm going to head back to Spokane."

"We'll fly back with you, dear. Richard, why don't you call the airport and see if we can get tickets for the three of us?"

"I appreciate it, Mom, but you've already been away from New York for too long. Nicole is probably going nuts with the twins and the new baby. I'll bet she's desperate to have you there to lend a hand." And hopefully Jenna's oldest sister wouldn't mind being used as an excuse.

"We can't just leave you to fend for yourself during this crisis," Lila said.

"It's not a crisis. It's a little blip on the screen. Besides, you've already got your tickets home."

"Tickets can be changed." Her father spoke up as they stepped onto the elevator, and Jenna patted his arm, offering a smile that she hoped was filled with confidence.

"They can be, but there's no need to change them. I haven't done anything wrong. The police are just pulling at straws—they're not going to find anything."

"I'm not worried about what they're going to find. I'm worried about you."

"Don't. I'm a grown woman, remember?"

"A grown woman and still my little girl." But her father didn't argue further as the elevator doors opened.

Jenna stepped out, her gaze drawn to the nurses' station where two uniformed officers waited. Her heart jumped, and if there hadn't been five people stepping off the elevator behind her, she would have turned tail and run.

Instead, she pasted a smile on her face and moved forward.

"Ms. Dougherty, it looks like you're feeling better." A young female officer stepped toward her, offering a brief smile.

"I am. Thank you."

"Good. We have a few questions we need to ask if you're up to it."

"I am."

"Are you sure, Jenna?" Nikolai stood beside her, his expression grim.

"I've got nothing to hide."

"How about we talk in your room, then?" The officer smiled again, but her eyes were hard, and Jenna knew she was already forming an assessment and deciding Jenna's guilt or innocence.

"That's fine. Mom, Dad, why don't you two go back to the hotel and get packed? I know your flight leaves in a few hours. Yours, too, Kane. I'll call you all as soon as I'm done here." She knew they'd protest, but she really didn't want her folks hanging around while the police gave her the third degree.

"We'll wait out here. You'll need a ride to the hotel when you're finished," Kane said, and the female officer shook her head.

"We'll be happy to give her a ride. You folks go ahead back to the hotel. It's best if we question Ms. Dougherty alone." It was an order. There was no doubt about that. Whether or not her family would obey it remained to be seen.

Jenna stepped into the room, pulling her IV pole along, her heart pounding way too fast and way too loudly. Could the officers see how nervous she was? She hoped not. The last thing she wanted to do was give them the impression that she had something to be nervous about.

Her legs were shaking, her mind fuzzy from the pain medicine she'd been given. Maybe answering questions *wasn't* a good idea. Before she could say as much, the second officer closed the door, sealing the three of them into the room together. Jenna winced at the sound, her pulse racing with anxiety. Should she send the officers away? Try to answer their questions? Refuse to answer them?

"Would you like to sit down before we begin?" The female officer pulled out a notebook, and Jenna did as she suggested, dropping into a chair.

"I hope this won't take too long, Officer. It's been a difficult day, and I'm not up to more than a few questions."

"A difficult day seems an understatement. You were at your friend's funeral reception when you were shot at, right?"

"I'm not sure if I was the target, but, yes, I was at Magdalena's funeral reception."

"You and Dr. Romero were close friends, weren't you?"

"Yes."

"Had you known each other long?"

"Since college."

"So, it's safe to say that you two have spent a lot of time together?"

"I wish I could say that was true, but Magdalena and I had only seen each other a handful of times in the past few years. She moved here after college, and I stayed in New York and then moved to Washington."

"But you went to Mexico together."

"I'm a physical therapist specializing in pediatrics. Magdalena asked me to take part in Team Hope."

"That's the group that runs medical clinics down in Mexico?"

"That's right."

"And Dr. Romero was the founder of the organization?"

"Yes, she coordinated several trips every year."

"I suppose she told you her reasons for doing so." The second officer, a tall, dark-eyed man in his twenties, spoke up, his expression bland. He looked bored, and Jenna didn't blame him. She'd been answering the same questions for a week, and her answers hadn't varied.

"She loved people. She had a heart for helping others. I don't think she needed any other reason than that."

"But she did have a young son. A little boy she left at home so that she could go serve others."

"Magdalena's love for her son and her service to others were not mutually exclusive."

"I'm sure there are a lot of mothers out there who would disagree with you." The male officer tapped his fingers on his thigh impatiently, and Jenna bit back a harsh retort.

"I think there are more who would agree."

"So, you think that she went to Mexico out of the goodness of her heart, to serve others and to help those who weren't as fortunate as she was?"

"Of course, I do." Jenna's voice rose, and she didn't bother to lower it.

"And this was your first trip to Mexico with her?"

"You know it was, and if you've got nothing to ask except the same questions I've already been asked a hundred times, then I'd prefer that you leave."

"Do you know that the DEA found illegal drugs in Dr. Romero's house?"

"Her husband told me."

"And did he also tell you that a large sum of money was deposited into her bank account a few days before she left for Mexico?"

"No."

"There was."

"Look, you've already decided Magdalena is guilty of drug trafficking. Everything you find and everything you hear is going to be used to prove your theory. There's nothing I can say that will change that."

"We haven't decided anything. We're simply gathering facts."

"What facts? You have a bunch of circumstantial evidence that means absolutely nothing." She knew she was losing her cool but couldn't make herself keep quiet, the heat of her anger chasing away the fuzziness in her head.

"Ms. Dougherty—"

A soft knock interrupted the officer's words and the door swung open. "Sorry to interrupt, but I grabbed a nurse and got the doctor to give her the go-ahead to unhook the IV. She'll be here in just a minute." Nikolai stepped into the room, and despite the apology, he didn't look at all sorry.

"We're in the middle of an interview, Mr....?"

"Jansen. Nikolai. And I'm sure there's nothing that you're saying that can't be said in front of me."

The male officer frowned, but the female officer simply shrugged. "You're a friend of Ms. Dougherty's?"

"Yes." He moved in close, his arm bumping Jenna's, and she was sure she smelled French fries and hamburgers. Two of her favorite foods.

She almost leaned in, inhaled deeply, let herself sink into the comfort of Nikolai's presence. Surprised, she stiffened her spine, forced herself to stay upright and focused. Obviously, anger hadn't completely chased the fuzziness from her brain.

"Were you part of the trip to Mexico, Mr. Jansen?" the officer asked.

"No."

"Then, if you'll wait out in the hall for just a moment, we'll be finished shortly."

The female officer offered a smile and turned her attention back to Jenna, obviously expecting that Nikolai would do as she'd asked.

"No."

"Pardon me?"

"I'm not leaving."

"The interview will move more quickly if it's conducted in private. I'm sure that you and Jenna understand that."

What Jenna understood was that she'd been asked the same questions over and over again during the past few days. What she understood was that answering those questions wasn't going to convince anyone of anything. While she hadn't expected Nikolai to stick around, she was glad he had, and there was no way she was going to make the interview any easier on the officers than she already had.

"Up until now, I've been happy to cooperate, but the questions you're asking are no different than the ones I've already answered. Maybe the interview would go more quickly if you asked some new ones."

"The questions we're asking are helping us paint a clearer picture of what went down in Mexico and will hopefully help us understand why it went down."

"I've already told the DEA what happened. I've already told the Mexican police. Now, I'm telling you. My friend and I went to Mexico on a medical mission trip. We were abducted, and my friend was murdered. There was no reason for it. Magdalena did nothing to warrant execution. She was an upstanding citizen, a wonderful mother, a great wife and a fantastic friend. She didn't deserve to die." To her horror, her voice broke and tears burned behind her eyes.

She hated crying.

Hated it.

"I think this interview is over." Nikolai put his arm around Jenna's shoulders, tugging her to his side. She went willingly, allowing his warmth to seep into her and ease the chill that she'd barely realized she was feeling.

"We only have a few more questions." The female officer persisted, not at all bothered by Jenna's distress.

"Nikolai is right. I can't answer any more questions."

"Perhaps tomorrow—"

"I'm flying home as soon as I can get a flight out of Houston."

"We don't recommend that."

"Because you'd prefer I be here when my house is searched?"

"We're gathering evidence, Jenna."

"Evidence regarding what?" Nikolai interjected. "No crimes have been committed except those that were committed against Jenna and her friend. How can searching Jenna's home help you solve those?" Nikolai walked to the door. Maybe he was hoping the police would follow him.

They didn't, of course.

"Dr. Romero had tens of thousands of dollars worth of illegal narcotics in her home. A few thousand dollars worth more were found in the hotel room she and Jenna were sharing."

"The drugs were found in the doctor's bags. What does that have to do with Jenna?"

"That's what we're trying to find out."

"You can try all you want, but you're not going to find anything." Jenna hoped. As much as she wanted to believe in the system, she was worried that whoever had planted drugs in Magdalena's house and in her bags would do the same in hers.

"I'm sorry it took me so long, Jenna. I had to get the doctor's..." A nurse appeared in the open door, her voice trailing off as she caught sight of the two officers. "Should I come back in a few minutes?"

"No. You're fine. Thanks." Jenna spoke quickly, anxious to get the IV out and leave the hospital. She needed some time to think.

"Are you sure? Because it really wouldn't be a problem to come back."

"I'm sure."

"All right, then. This will just take a minute. Come have a seat, dear."

"We'll wait out in the hall," the female officer said, and Jenna shook her head.

"I'd rather you didn't. I've had a long day, and I think I'm ready for it to be over."

"We'll call you in the morning then."

"That's fine." Though she planned to be long gone by then.

Both officers left, and Jenna sat on the edge of the bed as the nurse pulled the IV from her arm and pressed a Band-Aid into place. "There you are. It's as easy as that."

"Thank you."

"And here are the doctor's orders. I'll just give them to your husband to hold onto. Basically—"

"He's not my husband." Jenna cast a quick look in Nikolai's direction, sure her face was the color of ripe tomatoes.

"Oh. Sorry about that. I shouldn't have assumed."

"It's no problem." Jenna reached for the sheet, folded it in half without looking at it and stood.

"I'll just grab a wheelchair, and I'll be right back to get you out of here." The nurse bustled out of the room, and Jenna didn't think there was any reason to wait for her return.

"Ready to go?" She offered Nikolai a quick smile.

"You're not going to wait for your chariot?"

"Would you?"

"Not a chance." He grinned, and Jenna blinked. He looked younger when he smiled like that. More approachable. The kind of guy she'd have been drawn to in her other life.

But this wasn't her other life.

Things had changed. She'd changed.

"That's what I thought you'd say. Let's get out of here. The sooner I get back to the hotel and wash the hospital scent out of my hair, the happier I'll be."

"What hotel are you staying at?"

"The Sheraton. It's a few miles from Magdalena's place."

"I know it. My car is in the parking garage. You want to use my cell phone and let your parents know that you're on your way?" He put a hand on her upper back, his touch light. Somehow, though, she felt it more intensely than she'd felt anything in a long time.

She eased away, moving out into the hall, her heart beating just a little too quickly. After Ryan broke up with her, she'd promised herself that she wouldn't ever be so needy again.

And she *had* needed Ryan.

Bald, skinny, sallow-skinned from treatment, she'd felt anything but feminine in the months following chemotherapy.

She'd needed reassurance that she was still the woman she'd been before the first drop of poison dripped into her veins. What she'd gotten instead was the cold reality of Ryan's betrayal.

"Jen?" Nikolai stopped walking and looked into her face, his dark eyes filled with concern. "Are you sure you're up to this? Maybe it would be best to stay here."

"I'm fine. I was just...thinking."

"About?"

"Nothing important."

"If it's not important, then why are you thinking about it?"

"I've had enough questions thrown at me today, Nikolai. How about we just walk?" She started forward again, knowing that there was no good answer to what he'd asked. Even if she'd wanted to answer, she couldn't have. Why *was* she thinking about Ryan? After he'd broken the news that he no longer loved her, she'd pushed him out of her heart and out of her mind. Now, suddenly, after two years, she was thinking about him again.

And she didn't like it.

There were much more important things to think about. Like how she was going to prove Magdalena's innocence. How she was going to prove her own innocence. Those were things she'd better concentrate on if she planned to go back to the life she'd been living in Spokane.

And she did.

She could only hope that was God's plan, too.

One thing she'd learned during her fight against cancer was that all the plans in the world meant nothing unless God was in them. She could plot out a course for her life, one with a husband and kids. She could choose a career path. She could plan for a future, but only God knew what tomorrow would bring. As hard as that was to embrace, she'd done so during those difficult years. She'd embrace it now as well.

One moment at a time. One day at a time. That's how she'd deal with the new trouble she'd found herself in. God willing, she'd make it through and reclaim the life she'd fought so hard for.

EIGHT

Nikolai hadn't been born patient. As a kid, he'd been quick to use his fists to make a point. He'd fought hard to bring home food for his younger sisters and to protect them from the men their drug-addicted mother had often brought home. All that had changed the year he'd turned twelve and his mother had dropped her three children off at an orphanage. Left them there to survive or not.

Nikolai had learned to practice patience then. He'd learned to be quiet and to listen. He'd learned that time could speed up just as easily as it could slow down. He'd learned what it was to lose the people he loved the most, and he'd learned that he could survive the pain of it.

Yeah, he'd learned to practice patience, but dealing with the police while they questioned Jenna had just about driven him to the edge of reason.

He opened the car door for her, holding her elbow as she climbed in. Daylight had waned, and the parking garage was dimly lit, the sound of other hospital visitors echoing through the cement structure. Nikolai listened for other things. Furtive footfalls on pavement. The click of a gun safety being released. The slide of fabric or the soft huff of a breath. Someone had tried to kill Jenna just a few hours ago, and there was no reason to believe that person would be content to let her leave Houston alive.

The garage went quiet as he stepped around the car. The

sounds of people and conversation faded, the echoing tap of feet disappeared. Something sinister lay in the silence, and Nikolai turned, scanning the garage. He'd been caught off guard earlier. Like everyone else, he'd assumed that the Panthers had achieved their goal in murdering Magdalena and that Jenna was safe from harm.

He wouldn't be caught off guard again.

A shadow shifted in his periphery, and he turned as a man stepped from between two cars. Medium height. Medium build. Well-dressed and carrying a briefcase. Not someone Nikolai would normally have noticed. Not someone he would normally have thought of as a threat.

But these weren't normal circumstances, and everyone was a threat until proven otherwise.

"Hey!" The man called out, offering a quick wave and a brief smile. "I've locked myself out of my car, and my cell phone is in it. Can you give me a hand?"

"I'll call hospital security. They should be able to open the car for you."

"That would be great. Thanks." The man smiled again, moving closer, his green eyes feverishly bright. "It's just one of those days, you know?"

"Yeah." Nikolai pulled the cell phone from his pocket, pressing numbers without losing eye contact. There was nothing in the other man's gaze, just an intensity that Nikolai had seen in another city in another country in what sometimes felt like another lifetime.

"Once a day starts bad. It just keeps getting worse," the man said, his muscles tightening, giving his intentions away as he reached beneath his jacket.

Nikolai didn't wait to see what he was reaching for. He didn't question the instincts that had him diving across the distance that separated them, slamming the other man to the ground.

They landed with a crash, sliding across the pavement, Nikolai's cell phone clattering to the ground. He thought he heard a faint voice and hoped he'd connected to a 911 operator.

The guy wasn't muscular, but he had an unnatural strength that might have been fed by drugs or adrenaline or a combination of both.

"Let me go, man. Are you nuts?" The panted question would have made Nikolai hesitate if he hadn't been so sure of what he'd seen in the other man's eyes.

"No. And I'm not stupid, either." He strong-armed the guy onto his stomach, frisking him and pulling a gun from beneath his jacket.

"Hey!" The man twisted violently, bucking against Nikolai's hold.

"Don't give me a reason to use this." Nikolai pressed the gun into the other man's temple, smiling grimly as he immediately went still.

"You had no cause to attack me, man. Give me back my gun and let me out of here."

"You have a permit for the weapon?"

"Do you have a badge that gives you the right to ask me that?" He twisted again, and Nikolai pressed the gun a little harder into flesh.

"What's your name?"

"What's it to you?"

"It's a lot seeing as how you were planning to shoot me."

"I wasn't—"

"Nikolai?" Jenna called out, her feet tapping against the pavement as she moved toward him.

"Go back to the car." He didn't turn his attention from the gunman, couldn't afford to let himself be distracted.

"I'm going to get your phone and call the police."

"I already dialed 911. Get back in the car." The gunman stiffened, bucking hard against his hold, more desperate to escape now that he thought the police were on the way.

Jenna ignored his order, sidling past him and grabbing the phone. "Hello? Yes, we need the police."

"You can talk to the operator *in the car*." Nikolai took his eyes off the gunman just long enough to spear Jenna with a look he hoped would send her running.

She frowned and took a step back, but she didn't retreat. "A man with a gun tried to attack my friend. No one is hurt. The gunman is pinned to the ground."

The sound of sirens filled the garage, and the gunman jerked, his fist flying up and knocking the gun to the side. Nikolai slammed it into the man's temple, not bothering to hold back. "Don't. Move. You even breathe hard and it will be the last breath you ever take." He barked the words, and the gunman froze. Unlike Jenna, he seemed to understand the kind of trouble he was in.

A police cruiser raced into view, squealing to a stop a dozen yards away. The door swung open and an officer stepped out. Female. Dark hair. Definitely the same one who'd interrogated Jenna. "Mr. Jansen, please put the gun on the ground and keep your hands where I can see them."

"I don't think that's a good idea, Officer. This man will bolt if I give him half a chance."

"Who is he?" She moved toward him as her partner rounded the cruiser.

"That's what I was trying to find out. What's your name, pal?"

"I want a lawyer."

The officer ignored him, taking the gun from Nikolai, checking the safety and then handing it to her partner. "Let's bag this for evidence. We'll want to check it against the bullets that were found at the Romero house. Let's see if you've got any other weapons." She frisked the gunman, then slapped cuffs on his wrists and pulled him to his feet.

The guy still had a feverish look to his eyes, his face flushed and slack. "I said I want a lawyer."

"You'll get one. Read this guy his Miranda rights, will you, Joe?" She passed the gunman over to her partner who walked him to the cruiser, reading his Miranda rights as they went.

"Are either of you hurt?"

"Thanks to Nikolai, no." Jenna clutched Nikolai's cell phone in her fist, her face parchment pale.

"Did he fire the gun?"

"No, but he would have if he'd had a chance." Nikolai glanced at the gunman, wishing he could have a few minutes alone with the guy. His tactics wouldn't be legal, but he was pretty confident he could get the information he wanted.

"Unfortunately, we can't throw the book at him for something he hasn't done." The officer frowned.

"You can throw the book at him if the gun he was carrying matches the weapon used this afternoon."

"True. It's the same caliber, so we're halfway there."

"Let's hope we make it the rest of the way and get the guy thrown in jail where he belongs." Nikolai crossed the few feet that separated him from Jenna, but she didn't seem to notice. Her gaze was on the gunman who was being nudged into the backseat of the cruiser.

"I don't even know who he is."

"What's that?" The officer looked up from the notes she was scribbling.

"I've never seen him before in my life. What reason would he have for trying to kill me?"

"We'll question him and see what we can find out, but he's already asked for a lawyer, and I don't think we'll get much from him."

"Do you think…?" Jenna's voice trailed off, but Nikolai knew what she wanted to ask. Was the gunman Magdalena's murderer?

"That this guy is responsible for your friend's death? We're going to do everything we can to find out. Now, if you'll excuse me, the sooner we get our guy back to the station and get him that lawyer he's hollering about, the sooner we can start asking questions. Give me a call if you have any questions. Your case number is on the card." The officer handed

Nikolai a business card and offered one to Jenna as well. She took it, her movements wooden and tight.

"How long will it take for the ballistics test to be done?" she asked, her gaze jumping to the cruiser. Her eyes were deeply shadowed, her cheekbones high and sharp in what should have been a softly pretty face.

"If we get this gun back to the office soon, we may be able to have the results tonight. I'll call you as soon as it's complete."

"I appreciate that."

"No problem."

Jenna watched as the officer walked away, her expression blank.

What was she thinking?

That she'd never get her life back? That no matter what information the police received from their prisoner, she would never feel safe again?

"You okay?" Nikolai put a hand on her shoulder, and she stiffened, then relaxed beneath his touch.

"Yes, thanks to you. Again. You've saved my life three times now."

"Are we keeping track?"

"Of course." She offered a slight smile. "If we don't, I won't know how many times I'll need to save your life before we're even."

"Tit for tat, then?"

"That's an odd expression coming from a guy like you."

"What kind of guy would that be?"

She cocked her head to the side, studying him intently for a moment. "Tough. Hard. Not the kind of guy I'd imagine using the expression *tit for tat*."

"My mother uses it often. I suppose it's stuck in my head after seventeen years of hearing it."

"Only seventeen?"

"My parents adopted me when I was fourteen."

"And before that?"

"Before that I lived in another home and before that, another country." He took her arm, leading her back to the car. Talking about his past wasn't something he usually did. Not with his family. Not with the women he dated. The way he'd lived, the life he'd come from wasn't something that he shared.

"That explains your accent. I've been wondering."

"Have you?" He opened the car door, and Jenna met his eyes as she slid into the car, her cheeks pink.

"I'm sure people ask you about it all the time."

"Only women." And, really, only women he'd dated, but he didn't think Jenna would want to know that.

"I can't believe guys never ask. What about coworkers? Aren't they curious?"

"I was in the Marines for eleven years. The soldiers I worked with were more concerned with whether or not I could shoot than where I got my accent." He rounded the car, scanning the parking garage as he'd done before. Still on alert for trouble. Though this time he didn't think it would come.

"Are you going to make me ask?" Jenna asked as he got in the car.

"Ask what?"

"About the accent."

"Latvian. I lived there for the first twelve years of my life."

"And then?"

"I was adopted by an American family. That didn't work out, and I was put into foster care, then adopted by another family." The way he said it made it sound as if each transition had been as easy as falling asleep and waking up again. It hadn't been that way. Not by a long shot. It wasn't something he dwelled on, or even thought about much, but those years had been difficult. They'd honed him into the man he'd become. For better or for worse.

"That must have been hard."

"It was necessary and, in the long run, it was for the best."

"You love your family, then?"

"They loved me when no one else would. I owe them a lot. I'll do whatever it takes to repay them."

"Love doesn't demand payment, Nikolai."

"The demand doesn't come from the ones giving love, but from the ones receiving it. They are the ones who feel the burden to repay."

"Do you really think of it that way? As if returning love is a burden?"

"To understand how I think of it, you would have to have come from where I've been." He pulled out of the parking garage, not quite sure how they'd gone from discussing his saving Jenna's life to discussing his feelings for the Jansens. For the first three years after he'd been adopted by them, he'd refused to change his name or acknowledge that he was part of their family. They hadn't wavered in their devotion to him, and, over time, he'd come to believe that they truly cared for him.

"I guess that's how it always is," Jenna said quietly, and Nikolai wasn't sure if she were speaking more to herself or to him.

"What?"

"We can't know why people are the way they are until we understand where they've come from."

"So tell me, where have *you* come from, Jenna Dougherty? I'd have guessed you were the kind of woman to have married young and borne a busload of kids, but you've done neither of those things." Nikolai turned the conversation away from his past, more curious than he probably should be about Jenna's.

"That was the plan. I thought I'd marry straight out of college. Establish my career and then have a few kids. Sometimes, though, the things we plan aren't part of God's plan for us."

"What happened?"

"Leukemia happened. And then chemotherapy. And…"

"What?"

"Nothing worth talking about."

"Who was he?"

"Nobody. Just a guy I thought I loved and who was supposed to love me."

"That sounds like something worth talking about to me."

"That's because you didn't live it."

"Did you dump him or did he dump you?"

"You're awfully persistent, Nikolai."

"Only when I'm interested in something."

"Interested in what? A story that's two years old?"

"Interested in you."

"Why?"

"As you said, we can't understand a person until we know where she's come from."

"Maybe I should have asked why you'd want to understand me. Are you wondering how I got into this mess? Why a drug cartel as notorious as the Mexican Panthers wants me dead? Because if you are, knowing about my past won't help you. There's nothing there that would have brought this on."

"I know that. What I don't know is how a woman like you has managed to stay single for so long." The words slipped out before he could think better of them, and Nikolai wished he could grab them back.

What was he thinking, saying such a thing?

Obviously, Jenna wondered the same thing. She stiffened, her hands fisting in her lap. "It's easy to figure out, Nikolai. I tried the commitment thing. It didn't work out. I have no desire to try it again."

"I shouldn't have asked. It's none of my business."

"You're right, but since you saved my life, I guess I can forgive you for being nosy."

"Nosy is a good quality in P.I.s, and it's what's going to

help me help you." He pulled into the Sheraton parking lot, easing into a space close to the building.

"Just concentrate on proving Magdalena's innocence. I'll worry about keeping myself out of jail."

"It's not jail I'm worried about, Jenna. Do you think the guy who came after you today will be the last of the Panthers' henchmen?"

"I'm hoping so."

"Then you're hoping in vain."

"You can't know that. I've never had anything to do with the Panthers. They've got no reason to keep coming after me."

"Then why are they?" He asked the question though he knew Jenna had no answer. Neither did he, but he planned to find one.

"I don't know. Maybe the guy the police arrested will answer that question for us."

"Maybe."

But they both knew that wouldn't happen. The most they could hope for was that the police would prove that the gun the guy had been carrying was the same one used at the Romero house. Without that connection, he'd be out on the street in no time.

"I guess I'd better get moving. My family is probably wondering what's taking so long."

"I'll walk you in."

"That's not necessary, Nikolai."

"We both know it is." He got out of the car before she could argue, walking around and opening the door for her, inhaling the scent of vanilla mixed with the antiseptic hospital smell that seemed to cling to both of them.

Jenna grabbed his hand, allowing him to pull her from the car. Her hand was cool and dry, her skin silky against his palm. She'd clutched his hand earlier, clung to him as she'd faced the police. She did the same as they walked across the parking lot and into the building, the warmth of her touch searing through Nikolai, reminding him of childish dreams of a wife and a family and a happy home.

But a man like Nikolai could never live that dream. He'd known that for years, had accepted it just as he'd accepted his solitary life for what it was—part of who he was.

Still, as he pushed the elevator button and felt Jenna's hand tighten on his, he couldn't help wondering if time had changed him, if *God* had changed him enough so that he could shoot for the dream and try to make it a reality.

NINE

A 2:00 a.m. flight out of Houston was exactly what the doctor ordered. At least that's what Jenna told herself as she zipped her duffel, grabbed her purse and checked it for her passport and driver's license. Going home to her little house on the outskirts of Spokane, Washington, would do a lot to ease her stress. That would cut down on the headaches she'd been having. Fewer headaches would mean sleeping better, which would mean having a better appetite and, hopefully, improved blood counts. The last thing she wanted was another trip to the hospital and another round of medical tests.

In a few minutes the police escort Kane had insisted on would arrive and Jenna would be on her way home. She'd go back to the quiet life she'd been living before she'd agreed to accompany Magdalena to Mexico, but nothing would be the same. There was no way it could be.

Magdalena was dead.

The Mexican Panthers wanted Jenna to meet the same fate.

The police seemed determined to pin drug-crime convictions on Jenna.

And God was in control.

That was what Jenna's father had said before he'd kissed her goodbye and headed for the airport with Jenna's mother. It was what Jenna had repeated to Kane as she shooed him out of the hotel and into a cab an hour later.

She believed it. Probably more than she ever had before, but that didn't mean she wasn't scared.

She paced to the window, peering out into the darkness. As hard as she'd worked to convince her family to go back to their lives, she couldn't help wishing they were with her. A little conversation, some laughter—those things would go a long way in easing her tension.

She glanced at the clock, frowning. Her escort should have arrived. It was a forty-minute drive to the airport, and she didn't want to miss her flight. She grabbed the phone, dialed Officer Daniels's number and jumped as someone tapped on the door.

She tossed the phone back onto the receiver and hurried to the door. "Who is it?"

"Nikolai."

"What are you doing here?" she asked as she opened the door. He'd changed out of the suit he'd worn to the funeral, and Jenna caught a whiff of soap as he walked into the room.

"Kane called me. He told me that you managed to get a flight out of town."

"And you came to say goodbye?"

"Would that make you happy?" He sat down, his long legs stretched out, his arms folded over his chest. His biceps pulled at the soft fabric of his shirt and dark stubble shadowed his jaw. He looked strong and tough and perfectly capable of taking care of business, whatever that business might be.

"It's nearly midnight. You could have called and said goodbye rather than coming all the way over here."

"I thought we could ride to the airport together."

"I'm sure Kane told you that he asked Officer Daniels to give me a ride and escort me to the boarding gate."

"And I'm assuming he didn't tell you that I was coming along." He offered an easy smile.

"I haven't spoken to him since he left for the airport."

"He called me just before he boarded. I'm sure he planned to call you once he landed."

"He asked you to ride to the airport with me?" That didn't surprise Jenna. Her parents and brother had been reluctant to leave her in Houston for even a few hours. It had taken plenty of convincing to get them checked out of the hotel and on their flights home.

"No. He just wanted to let me know that you were leaving town. Everything else was my idea."

"Everything?" Jenna wasn't sure what that meant, but she had a feeling she wasn't going to like it.

"I'm going to escort you to Spokane."

She'd been right. She didn't like it. "That's completely unnecessary."

And completely unacceptable.

In the worst days of her cancer treatment, when she'd desperately needed Ryan's support, she'd felt the distance between them growing and had known that the love she'd believed in was a lie.

Nikolai was different. He was a man who'd draw closer during a crisis, who'd give whatever was necessary without thought to his own needs. She'd seen that over and over again in the past week. And she'd found herself clinging to him. Holding on when she should have backed away and let go.

"You don't think so?"

"I'm not your responsibility, Nikolai. So, no, I don't."

"Then we see things differently."

"I appreciate your concern, and I know you're trying to help, but I have to keep living my life the way I always have."

"Do you think that will make your troubles go away?" He watched her through narrowed eyes, his dark gaze skimming over her white T-shirt and peasant skirt, assessing her in a way that made her cheeks heat and her heart pound. She turned away, staring out the window and willing her pulse to slow.

"No, but moving on with my life will make me feel more in control."

"I understand." Fabric rustled as he stood, but Jenna didn't turn to face him. She didn't want to see the interest in his eyes. More than that, she didn't want to respond to it.

"Then you'll understand why I'll have to insist that you not do this. You've done enough for me already. I won't ask you for more."

"You've asked me for nothing. I'm worried about you, Jenna. I want to make sure you make it home safely. Is that so difficult to accept?"

"Yes. It is."

"Why?" He cupped her shoulders and urged her around, his dark eyes searching her face.

"Because, I don't want to go back to depending on anyone."

"And being disappointed?" His hands fell away, but their warmth lingered.

"That, too."

"I won't disappoint you, Jenna. If you need me, I'll be there for you."

"You don't get it, Nik—"

A soft tap interrupted her words, and she hurried to the door, glad for a reason to end the conversation.

"I'll get it." Nikolai stepped in front of her, his broad shoulders blocking her view. "Who's there?"

"Officer Daniels."

Nikolai opened the door, stepping aside to let the officer in. "Thanks for coming."

"No problem. I planned to come out anyway. We finished questioning our gunman, and we were finally able to get his identity. His name is Brent Lamar. He's a known affiliate of the Mexican Panthers. The gun he was carrying was a match to the weapon that fired the bullets we found at the Romero house."

"Did he give you any reasons?" *For wanting me dead* was on the tip of Jenna's tongue, but she couldn't make herself say it.

"He's not saying much of anything, but we're working under

the assumption that he had orders from the Panthers. We're hoping to work out a plea bargain. Lesser charges in exchange for information, but I can't promise he'll go for it."

"We can pray he does," Nikolai said, lifting Jenna's duffel bag and carrying it to the door.

"Prayers are about all we've got right now. The good news is, we don't think you have to worry about the Panthers anymore. Word on the street is that they're lying low for a while."

"And you believe that?" Nikolai obviously didn't.

"Generally, our informants are on the money." Officer Daniels stepped into the hall, and Jenna followed, Nikolai close on her heels.

"Your informants are also criminals. They would tell you anything if they were paid enough to do it."

"You have a point, but I don't think that's the case this time. The DEA has confirmed that the Panthers are staying in Mexico. There hasn't even been a whisper of a hit being put out on Jenna."

A hit being put out on her? Jenna would have laughed at the idea if it weren't so horrifying. "Why would there be? I haven't done anything to get on their hit list."

"And, yet, there have been two attempts on your life. Maybe they think you know something. Or maybe it's simply a matter of pride. You did escape their stronghold, after all. And that's unheard of." Officer Daniels shrugged.

"I should send them a note of apology and ask them to leave me alone." She tried to smile, but it fell flat.

"How about we just get you on the plane home?" Nikolai took her hand, squeezing softly. She knew she should pull away, but she didn't. It felt too good to have his support.

"Are you coming to the airport with us, Jansen? If so, you'll have to ride in the back of the cruiser."

"I'm flying to Spokane. I'll follow you to the airport."

"Sounds good. Do you want to ride with me, Jenna? Or will you be riding with Nikolai?"

She *should* ride with Officer Daniels, but for reasons she didn't want to admit, even to herself, she decided against it. "I'll ride with Nikolai."

If he was surprised, Nikolai didn't show it.

"Sounds good." Officer Daniels pressed the elevator call button. "I'll escort the two of you into the airport and to the security gate. Once you're past the gate, you should be safe. We have contacted the Spokane County Police and the Washington State Police. They're aware of what's happened here and will offer whatever assistance you might need."

"Before or after they search my house and decide if I'm a drug dealer?" The question slipped out, and Jenna bit her lip to keep from saying more. Officer Daniels had been more than kind, and Jenna's rudeness was poor payment for that.

"I understand how you must feel, but I hope you understand that we have to pursue every avenue when we're investigating a case."

"What case? The one against the Mexican Panthers or the one against Magdalena?"

"She was your friend, Jenna, but that doesn't mean she didn't commit a crime." Officer Daniels's sympathetic tone did nothing to make Jenna feel better.

She didn't argue, though. She'd said all she would about Magdalena's innocence. Until she was able to prove it, she'd keep her thoughts to herself.

The night had grown chilly, the crisp spring air heavy with moisture. Shadows drifted across the pavement as Officer Daniels walked them to Nikolai's car. A cool breeze whipped at Jenna's hair, and she shivered, wishing she hadn't shoved her jacket into the duffel bag.

"Cold?" Nikolai slid an arm around her waist, pulling her up against his side. His warmth seeped through her T-shirt and his scent surrounded her, a mix of soap and masculinity that Jenna couldn't ignore no matter how much she tried.

"No."

"Then why are you shivering?"

Because she *was* cold.

And scared.

And tired.

And being near Nikolai was too much of a distraction and a temptation.

She frowned as he opened the car door. "I don't think this is a good idea."

"What?" His arm slipped from her waist, his breath ruffling her hair as he reached in the car to grab a pile of papers that lay on the passenger seat. The scent of mint seemed to fill the car, and Jenna's thoughts jumped back a week to the moment Nikolai had walked into her life and pulled her from the brink of death. He'd smelled of mint and leather, and his hands had been gentle as he'd touched her arms. She'd been too terrified to notice more than that, but those things had stuck in her mind and filled her dreams.

"Your driving me to the airport and escorting me to Spokane. You heard what Officer Daniels said. The Panthers aren't a threat any longer."

"You believe that?"

"I want to."

"Yeah, me, too. But I don't. There's something going on that we don't understand, Jenna. Until we know what it is, you can't afford to take chances." He closed the door and walked around the car, and Jenna knew he was right.

She couldn't afford to take chances and that should have made her eager to have an escort home.

And she *was* eager. Maybe even too eager. The fact was, spending more time with Nikolai wouldn't be a hardship and that worried her. She had a good life to go home to. A predictable life that didn't pose any risk to her health or her heart. That was the way she wanted it.

At least that's what she'd been telling herself for the better part of two years.

But maybe predictable was boring and maybe taking

risks was the only way to truly find what was missing from her life.

Missing?

She scowled, not liking the direction of her thoughts, and she was still scowling as Nikolai got into the car and started the engine.

"You look unhappy," he said as he pulled behind Officer Daniels's police cruiser.

"I'm not."

"Then why do you look as if you'd like to bite someone's head off?"

"It's just been one of those days."

"It seems to me that it's been one of those weeks."

"That, too."

"Things will get better."

"Good to know, since I don't think they can get any worse."

"That's the spirit." Nikolai patted Jenna's knee, his palm warm through the fabric of her skirt. She could hear the smile in his voice, could feel herself slipping into dangerous territory, allowing herself the luxury of companionship and friendship and maybe something more.

She'd had those things with Ryan. Believed in them as much as she'd believed in forever. When it ended, she'd known she never wanted to feel that way again.

And now she was in a car, riding toward the airport with a man she knew could turn her life upside down.

It wasn't a smart move.

Not smart at all.

Her head knew it, but her heart didn't seem to care.

Jenna bit back a sigh, her gaze on the dark road and the police car leading them to airport. She had enough on her plate. She didn't need to waste time worrying about Nikolai. There were more pressing things to deal with. Like the fact that the Mexican Panthers might still want her dead. Like the fact that the police seemed convinced that Magdalena had been involved in drug trafficking. Like the gigantic mess that she'd found herself entangled in.

No, she didn't have time to waste worrying about the way Nikolai made her feel. Feelings, after all, were fleeting and could change as quickly as the weather. Jenna had learned that the hard way, and she wouldn't forget it. Only God was constant, and it was He she needed to put her trust in. That was a lesson from childhood, and one she'd come back to over and over again while she'd fought cancer. She'd cling to it now as well, and it would be enough.

It had to be.

There was nothing else.

Sure, Nikolai was attractive and interesting. Sure he seemed caring and strong. Sure, Jenna could imagine depending on him. She could even imagine losing her heart to him.

What she couldn't imagine was doing any of those things and coming out unscathed. She'd had her heart broken once, and she wouldn't let it happen again. All she had to do was keep that in mind and she'd be just fine.

TEN

It took forty minutes to reach the airport, and by the time they arrived, Jenna had managed to push aside her misgivings. Nikolai could travel to Spokane with her or not. Either way, she'd be just fine. She was tough—she'd proven that over and over again. Whatever happened, she'd weather the storm and grow stronger because of it.

They parked in the long-term parking garage, and Officer Daniels motioned for them to get in the police cruiser. "I'll drive you to the terminal. There's no sense taking chances."

"I thought you said Jenna was no longer in danger."

"I said that we had good reason to believe the Panthers have lost interest in her. That doesn't mean we should throw caution to the wind."

"You want to take the front or backseat?" Nikolai asked.

"I've never ridden in the back of a police car, so I guess I'll sit there."

"You sure? I've been in the back plenty, and I can tell you for sure that it's not much to write home about."

"Should I ask how you wound up in the backseat of a police cruiser?"

"Let's just say, I had a misspent youth. It's only by the grace of God that I didn't end up with a criminal record and a cell in the state penitentiary," Nikolai responded as Jenna slid into the backseat. He leaned in and set her duffel bag on the floor, his arm brushing her leg, his masculine scent surrounding her. Her pulse leaped, her heart skipping a beat as she met his eyes.

"A misspent youth? Now you've made me curious."

"That makes two of us."

"What do you mean?"

"Simply that there are things about you that I'd like to know, too. Fortunately, we'll have plenty of time to get to know each other on the way to Spokane." He closed the door, and Jenna was sure she should say something when he got into the car. Maybe tell him that she knew everything about him that she wanted to know, or that he had no reason to be curious about her. But she wasn't sure either of those things were true, and she kept silent as he settled into the front seat and Officer Daniels drove them to the terminal.

Despite the late hour, the airport bustled with activity. People milled around ticket counters and stood waiting by doors. Flanked by Nikolai and Officer Daniels, Jenna felt safe enough, though she wondered how easy it would be for one of the Mexican Panthers to enter the airport with a gun or a knife or some other deadly weapon.

Just the thought was enough to send her heart rate soaring.

"Do you want to check your duffel?" Nikolai held her bag and his own duffel, and she shook her head.

"I'll carry it on the plane."

"And you already have your boarding pass printed out?" Officer Daniels asked.

"Yes."

"Sounds like the two of you can go straight to the boarding gate. I'll walk you to the security gate, and we'll say goodbye there." Officer Daniels sounded as anxious to get things moving as Jenna was.

"I appreciate your taking the time to escort us here." Jenna offered a smile as she pulled the boarding pass from her purse, took her driver's license from her wallet and walked toward the security gate.

"It was no problem. Just make sure you check in with the Spokane Police once you arrive. They'll want to meet with you in the next day or two."

It sounded more like an order than a request. Had they already searched Jenna's house? Had they found something? Just the thought made Jenna physically ill. She'd always believed that living an upright and law-abiding life would be enough to keep her out of trouble with the law.

Apparently, she'd been wrong.

"I'll do that."

"We may have more questions for you. If you plan to move or to change phone numbers, please let us know so that we can contact you if necessary."

"I'm not sure she legally has to do that, Officer." Nikolai pulled out his boarding pass and ID, offering Officer Daniels a smile that was anything but friendly.

"She's a witness to a crime, Mr. Jansen. I'm sure you understand how important it is for us to keep in contact with her."

"What I understand is that you suspect her of drug activities, even though you have no evidence to link her to a crime."

"As I've said before—" Officer Daniels began, but Jenna didn't think she could listen to a rehash of the same tired points.

"I'll keep you informed if there are any changes in my contact information, but I doubt there will be."

Officer Daniels nodded and fished a business card from his pocket. "If you have any questions or if you remember anything that you think will help our case, give me a call."

"I will." She shoved the card in her pocket, not sure what case he was referring to. Did he think she'd suddenly remember that Magdalena had been involved in drug trafficking? Or did he think she'd remember something about her time in Mexico that would help the police figure out why Jenna had been targeted for death?

"We'd better go." Nikolai put a hand on her arm, his fingers curving around her biceps. He had large hands. Nice hands.

And hands were something that Jenna always noticed about people. Nikolai's palms were broad, his fingers long. There were calluses on his palms and scars on his knuckles. He worked hard, and his hands told the story of it. Ryan's hands had been much smaller, his palms rough and often moist.

And why Jenna was even thinking about them, she didn't know.

"Jenna!" A masculine voice called from somewhere behind them, and Jenna turned, surprised to see John rushing toward her.

"John, what are you doing here?"

"Thank goodness I caught you before you left."

"Is everything okay? Is Benjamin okay?" Benjamin whose dark eyes and black hair were just like his mother's. Just the thought of something happening to him made Jenna light-headed. She swayed, clutching Nikolai's arm, and not caring about what that said about her and her needs.

"He's fine. I just had no idea you were going to leave today. I thought you planned to stay until Wednesday." John frowned, shifting from one foot to the other, his eyes shadowed.

"After what happened today, I decided it was best to go home. I did call your house and left a message with your mother."

"I know. I just got it. Today has been crazy, and I've barely had time to think." He ran a hand over his hair, and Jenna was sure it was trembling.

"Is everything okay, John?" She took a step toward him, stopping when he held up a hand.

"No. How can it be?"

"Are you upset that I'm leaving? I thought that with your parents here…"

"Upset? Of course not. You have to do what's best for you. It's just that I'd hoped we could spend some time together. I'd like to know more about Magdalena's time in Mexico. There are so many questions I haven't been able to ask."

"You can call me anytime. You know that, right?" She took

his hand, squeezing gently, her throat tightening as he offered a sad smile.

"You were her best friend, Jen. Having you around makes me feel as if a part of her is still here. I guess I was just hoping that would last a little longer."

She hadn't thought of it that way, hadn't even considered that sticking around might help John adjust to the reality of life without Magdalena. "I thought that with your parents here, you were doing okay. Maybe I should have thought a little harder."

"My parents knew Magdalena, but they were never as close to her as you were. I would have loved to spend a few days reminiscing with you. I'm sorry that the last few days have been too busy for us to get together."

"You had a lot going on. I understood that."

"Still, I should have made more time. I would have, if I'd realized we wouldn't have it after the funeral." He smiled again, shifting from foot to foot nervously. In the years she'd known him, Jenna had never thought of John as anything but calm and cool. No matter what the circumstances, he'd always maintained an aloof distance and emotional detachment. Obviously, Magdalena's death had changed that.

"We both should have tried harder to connect, but I think Magdalena's death was such a shock that neither of us were thinking straight. Maybe in a few weeks, I can come back. I'd love to see Benjamin again."

"A couple weeks would be nice, but my mother suggested another option."

"Your mother?"

"I told her how bad I felt that I'd pretty much ignored you these past few days. She suggested that she and my father move into the spare room, and you could stay in the guest suite."

"That's a nice idea, but I already have my ticket home."

"We'll pay for a ticket out on Wednesday, as you originally planned."

"I…" Jenna didn't know what to say. She'd had her heart set on returning to Spokane but she wasn't sure if she could look John in the eye and say no.

"I know there's been some trouble with the police." He glanced at Officer Daniels. "It may be easier to answer their questions if you stay in Houston, and I'll be happy to hire a lawyer for you if you need it."

"Lawyer?" The thought hadn't even occurred to her, but now that John mentioned it, she wasn't sure she could get it out of her mind.

"Maybe I'm out of line suggesting it."

"If I need a lawyer, I'll hire one myself." But she hoped she wouldn't need one.

"Understood, but at least let me give you some names, okay? I'd offer to represent you myself, but I think I'm too close to things, and I doubt I'd have the objectivity that is needed to win."

Win what? Did John really think Jenna would be arrested and tried for drug trafficking? She wanted to ask, but didn't dare. Not with Officer Daniels standing a few feet away.

"Jenna, if we're getting on that plane, we'd better get moving." Nikolai interrupted, his dark eyes focused on John.

"All right. I'll give you a call when I get to Spokane, John."

"Fine. That's fine. There was one more thing, though. Another reason I'd hoped you would stay."

"What's that?"

"Magdalena's lawyer requested that you be at the reading of the will. It's scheduled for tomorrow afternoon. I should have mentioned it days ago, but it slipped my mind what with all the funeral plans and police interviews."

"The reading of her will? Magdalena had a will?"

"My wife had very specific ideas about what should happen to her home and her family if she died. She had a lawyer draw up a will last year, and I believe you're mentioned in it."

"Oh." That was all Jenna could manage.

"Of course, you don't have to be there. The lawyer can contact you at home, but I think Magdalena would have liked the idea of all the people she loved gathered in one room, listening to her last wishes. I could probably get you a ticket to Spokane the following day, so you really wouldn't be putting your trip home off for more than forty-eight hours."

It was a trump card, and he knew it. Like John, Jenna could imagine Magdalena carefully planning the moment when those she loved most would gather to hear her last words to them. "All right. I'll stay."

"Are you sure? I don't want you to feel pressured into it."

"I do, but not by you. Magdalena would have wanted us to be together when the will was read." And Jenna would respect her friend's wishes. Home would be there in another few days, but the opportunity to honor Magdalena one last time would not be.

"Are you sure about this, Jenna?" Nikolai asked quietly, his expression guarded. Whatever he was thinking about John's appearance and his plea was well hidden.

"No more sure than I have been of anything these past few days, but I do know Magdalena would have wanted me there."

"And you'll stay at my place?" John seemed more relaxed now that he'd posed his question and gotten his answer.

"As long as your parents won't be put out."

"Of course they won't be. As I said, it was my mother's idea. Come on. Let's see if we can retrieve your luggage before they put it on the plane, and then I'll drive you home."

"That's all the luggage I have." She gestured to the duffel Nikolai held.

"Great." John reached to take the bag, but Nikolai didn't release his hold.

"I'll walk you out to your car." He didn't sound happy, and Jenna wanted to ask what was wrong. She met his eyes instead, trying to read the truth there.

"I'm right outside these doors. Probably getting ticketed for parking in a tow-away zone."

"I'll come along, too," Officer Daniels said, and Jenna felt like a well-protected prisoner as she followed John to the exit.

A black BMW stood in the tow-away zone, and John opened the passenger door. "You can toss the duffel in the trunk, Nikolai." He pushed a button on his key chain, and the trunk opened. Then he rounded the car and got into the driver's seat.

Jenna knew she should get in the car and let him take her back to his place, but she felt uncomfortable and just a little uneasy, and she hesitated, waiting as Nikolai put the duffel in the trunk and closed it.

"Are you sure this is what you want?" He moved close, and Jenna was sure she saw her uneasiness reflected in his eyes.

"It's what Magdalena wanted."

"And as sad as it is, she's gone. Make the decision for you, not for her."

"I'm not sure I can do that."

"What is holding you here? Your friend or her husband?"

"I barely know John," Jenna said, shooting a quick glance into the car. John had started the engine and was tapping his fingers to the radio.

"That's not what I meant."

"Then what did you mean?"

"That John fed you a guilt trip, and you swallowed it."

"He's beside himself with grief, Nikolai. Can you blame him for wanting to have someone who knew and loved Magdalena around?"

"He has his son, his parents, his friends. Why is he insisting on also having you?"

"Because Magdalena and I were as close as sisters."

"Maybe."

"What other reason could he have?" Jenna glanced at Officer Daniels who stood a few feet away.

"I don't know. Perhaps he's just the kind of person who likes to manipulate others."

"That's a horrible thing to say."

"Even if it's true?"

"It isn't. Magdalena would never have married someone like that."

"How well did she know him when they married?"

It was a good question. A fair question. And the fact was, John had swept Magdalena off her feet. They'd met in college, dated for just a few months before they'd become engaged and had been married less than a year later. That wasn't something Jenna planned to share, though. Not while John sat in the car waiting and Officer Daniels stood pretending not to listen. "How about we discuss this another time?"

"I'll pick you up tomorrow morning and take you to breakfast. We'll chat then."

"I—"

"Is nine o'clock too early?"

She should say it was. Even better, she should tell him that she wouldn't have breakfast with him at all. "No, nine o'clock is fine."

"Good." He grinned, flashing straight white teeth and a dimple that Jenna had never noticed before.

"I'll see you then." She turned, but he grabbed her hand before she could get in the car, leaning in close, speaking just loudly enough for Jenna to hear.

"If you need me, call. Do you have a pen and paper?"

"Just a pen." She dug it out of her purse, and he took it, turning her hand over and writing on her palm. The pen point tickled her skin as he scribbled his number.

"Copy it onto paper when you get to his place."

"All right."

"I don't trust that guy, so don't spend a lot of time alone with him."

"What do you mean?"

"Just a gut feeling. He's got more on his mind than the reading of the will and reminiscing about his wife. Stay safe, okay?"

"I will."

He nodded, hesitating for a moment longer, then walked away.

Jenna watched until he disappeared from sight, feeling more lonely with every step he took. It would have been easy to call out to him. To tell him that she'd changed her mind, that she didn't want to go back to John's showy house and his quietly stuffy parents.

But she didn't.

"You ready, Jenna?" John called out, and she nodded, turning back to the car, offering a brief wave at Officer Daniels as she got into the BMW.

Classical music poured from the radio, the sound doing nothing to soothe Jenna's raw nerves. She'd planned to be on the way home by now. Instead, she was heading back to the house where she'd nearly been killed.

She hoped she'd made the right choice.

She prayed she had.

But she didn't know.

And that scared her more than she wanted to admit.

ELEVEN

Nikolai paced the living room of his small apartment, watching as the second hand of the clock slowly made its circuit. One minute. Two. Three. Time seemed to pass in excruciatingly slow moments, and there was nothing he could do to speed it up.

It was going to be a very long night.

He walked into the kitchen and pulled a cold soda from the refrigerator. It wasn't something he drank often, but it hit the spot when what he really craved was a cold beer.

A cold beer and a cigarette. The two went hand in hand, and both were part of his life before.

Before the bomb that had nearly killed him.

Before the months he'd spent in a VA hospital.

Before he'd realized that he wanted more out of life than black lungs and a pickled liver. He wanted relationships. He wanted connection. He wanted to live life without booze to numb the experience.

Now, Nikolai chewed mint gum and drank soda. He faced life's pain head-on and poured his heart out to God instead of pouring his drug of choice down his throat. That's the decision Nikolai had made when he'd left the VA hospital. Nearly two and half years later, he hadn't veered from it.

Sometimes, though, he was tempted.

This was definitely one of those times.

He pulled open the fridge, scanning the shelves and

frowning at the meager pickings. He needed to go shopping, but it was a chore he hated. Too many people. Too much noise. He liked solitude and silence. Though right about now, he would have gladly faced airport crowds and noise to get Jenna out of John Romero's house.

Something wasn't right about the guy. Nikolai couldn't put his finger on what it was, but he didn't like the man. Or maybe he simply didn't like the fact that Romero had manipulated Jenna into doing what she didn't want to do.

He grabbed a piece of cheese from the fridge, dropped it onto whole wheat bread and glanced at the clock again. Too early to do much of anything, but that didn't mean there was nothing he could do. He carried the sandwich to his desk, booted up his computer and typed Romero's name into the search engine. The guy was mentioned several times in recent newspaper stories about Magdalena's death. "Her grieving husband, John Romero…" seemed to be the catchphrase of every reporter in Houston.

Was he grieving?

There were as many ways to grieve as there were people, but in Nikolai's mind John had been more concerned with showing off his home and his wealth than he'd been in remembering his wife. Perhaps that was simply the guy's way of coping with his grief. Or maybe Romero didn't miss his wife nearly as much as the rest of the world seemed to.

What had the couple's relationship been like?

Did John benefit from Magdalena's death in any way?

An unsettling thought, but one Nikolai needed to check into.

He typed Magdalena's name into the computer, curious about the woman that Jenna seemed so determined to defend. There were several articles about her death. Most touched on the investigation into drug trafficking and mentioned that Magdalena had been murdered execution-style. There were broad hints about the kind of activities that might have put her in danger. Less recent articles painted the doctor in a more positive light. Philanthropist. Healer. Friend to the friendless. Those were the kinds of things reporters had said before her death.

Which was the truth?

His cell phone rang as he clicked on an article about Magdalena's medical outreach to rural areas of Mexico. Surprised, he glanced at his watch. Three-thirty in the morning was an odd time for someone to call. The number was unlisted, and he lifted the phone, pressing the receiver to his ear. "Jansen, here."

"Nikolai? It's me."

He didn't need to ask who. He knew Jenna's voice almost instinctively, and he stood, grabbing his jacket and keys. "What's wrong?"

"Nothing." Her voice broke, and Nikolai opened his apartment door. Whatever was going on, he wasn't going to wait around for her to start screaming for help.

"Then why does it sound like you're crying?"

"I'm not." She sniffed, making a lie of the words.

"I'm coming over."

"No. That's not why I called."

"Then why did you?" He jogged to his car, climbed in and started the engine.

"I...shouldn't have." She sniffed again. Sad rather than scared. That's how she sounded, and Nikolai knew there was no real need to drive over to the Romero house.

Except that Jenna was there, and she sounded like she could use a friend. He knew how that felt. How easily memories could fill the mind during the darkest hours of the night. "I'll be there in fifteen minutes."

"Don't come. I shouldn't have called you. I don't even know why I did."

"Fifteen minutes," he repeated, hanging up the phone.

She could tell him as many times as she wanted that she didn't need him to come, that she didn't want him to come, but he wouldn't believe it. There were things that only someone who'd experienced them could understand. Walking through enemy fire and surviving, seeing a comrade fall—Jenna had done those things in a different way than Nikolai had, but he still understood her fears and her guilt. He knew what it was like to lie in bed at night and think about the men and women who hadn't survived. It was a heavy burden to bear.

He parked in front of the Romeros' driveway, scanning the darkened windows. A guest suite was usually in the basement of the house, but the Romero place was immense, and Nikolai figured it could be just about anywhere.

He got out of the car, walking across the dark front yard. No dog barked. No sign announced an alarm system. It seemed inconceivable that a house the size of this one had no security system, but there was no indication that the Romero family had one.

Despite Officer Daniels's assertion that Jenna was out of danger, Nikolai was worried. Until they knew why she'd been targeted for death, they couldn't be sure that the threat was really past. It was best if everyone involved kept that in mind, and Nikolai had every intention of reminding Romero of it when he saw him next.

Yellow crime scene tape cordoned off the porch, and Nikolai bypassed the area. No motion detecting lights flicked on, and the yard remained dark as he moved past the French doors. At the corner of the house a dim light shone faintly through a curtained window. He tapped on the glass. Jenna would look out, or someone else would. Either way worked.

A few seconds later, the curtain in a window to his left moved, opening just enough for someone on the other side to peek out. Nikolai offered a quick wave, stepping closer as the curtains opened wider. The room beyond was dark, but Jenna's pale face was unmistakable, her frown as clear as moonlight on a still pond.

She fumbled with the lock, then opened the window, her face pressing against the screen as she whispered. "I told you not to come."

"Did you think I'd listen?"

She hesitated, then shook her head. "I guess not."

"Can I come in?"

"There's a door on the side of the house. Meet me there."

Nikolai did as she asked, walking around the corner of the house and waiting at a door that must have been a private entrance to the guest suite. Windows flanked either side of the door, and Nikolai saw movement in the darkness beyond. A light spilled out onto the small stoop where he stood, and the door swung open.

"You shouldn't have come, Nikolai," Jenna said as she stepped aside and let him in.

"Why not?"

"Because it's four in the morning, and we should both be sleeping."

"But we aren't."

"No. I guess we're not. Would you like some coffee? I've got a fresh pot brewing."

"No. Thanks."

"Then how about some juice or water?" She walked into a small living room, gesturing for Nikolai to sit down. Like the rest of the Romero house, the guest suite was well-equipped. The living room opened into an eat-in kitchen that sported granite countertops and stainless steel appliances. A few pricey pieces of furniture created an upscale, showy feel that Nikolai knew was absolutely intended.

"I'm fine. Thanks." He settled onto a recliner, watching as Jenna walked into the kitchen. She'd changed into loose flannel pajama bottoms and a long-sleeved T-shirt that hung on her narrow frame. Freckles dotted her nose and cheeks, and her lips were a subtle pink. There was nothing ostentatious or showy about her, but somehow she seemed to fit perfectly into this upscale home.

She poured a cup of coffee and carried it into the living room, her movements stiff, her expression guarded. "I'm sorry I called you, Nikolai. I don't know what got into me."

"No?"

"I just…being here is difficult."

"You mean knowing that Magdalena isn't here with you?"

"Something like that." She smiled, taking a sip of coffee and placing it on a marble coaster. "What's weird is that I can't really picture Magdalena in this place."

"You mean in the guest suite?"

"I mean in the house. She didn't believe in pouring money into material things." She glanced around the room, her brow furrowed.

"The house says something different about her."

"I guess so. Maybe that's what's bothering me. None of this seems real. Not this fancy house or John's fancy car. Not the housekeeper or the catered reception after the funeral. Magdalena wouldn't have wanted any of this." She bit her lip and turned away, walking to a gas fireplace. A large picture hung above it—an impressionist painting of a field of flowers whose subtle colors blended into the décor. Jenna stared at it for a moment, her arms hugging her waist.

"It's okay." Nikolai walked to her side, not touching her. Just being there. Offering her what little comfort he could.

"No. It's really not. She's never coming back to this house or her husband or her son. Why? That's what I keep asking myself. It's why I can't sleep. That and…" She shook her head, and rubbed the back of her neck.

"You're here and she's not?"

She nodded, and Nikolai put a hand on her shoulder, felt the tautness of her muscles. She was holding her emotions in, bottling them up tight. It was another thing that he understood, another thing they had in common.

"Sometimes that is the hardest thing of all to accept." He spoke quietly, his hand sliding from her shoulder to the nape of her neck. Smooth skin and silky hair, the sweet scent of vanilla drifting around him. For a moment Nikolai forgot that his purpose was to comfort Jenna. For a moment he forgot that she was a woman he'd known for less than a week, a woman who'd been through too much.

She met his gaze, her eyes widening, her pulse racing beneath his fingers. She felt what he did. The tug of awareness. The sudden reality that they were a man and a woman standing alone in a quiet room.

He could have easily lost himself in the moment, let the feeling grow between them until neither could deny it. But Jenna deserved more than that. She deserved time to grieve for her loss, to accept it.

When she stepped away, he let her go, his hand falling to his side.

"I wish I could have saved her. I wish she'd come walking through the door, asking me what I was doing entertaining a man after hours." A tear slipped down her cheek, and she brushed it away impatiently.

"Would she have?"

"She was that kind of person. All about rules and propriety and living life the right way. Ask anyone, and you'll hear the same thing."

"Perhaps that was her downfall." Nikolai spoke the thought aloud, and Jenna nodded, thick strands of hair falling across her forehead.

"I've been thinking the same thing. If she knew something that could have caused trouble for the Panthers, that might have been enough to get her killed."

"What could she have known? That's the question we must ask ourselves. The Mexican Panthers have been around for decades. One American woman would not have had access to the sort of information that could have stopped their production and distribution. Why risk bringing the DEA down on their organization by murdering a U.S. citizen?"

"I hadn't thought of that." Jenna's eyes were dark-rimmed, her skin drawn tight against her cheekbones.

"I'm sure the police have. That's why they are so determined to believe Magdalena was trafficking in illegal drugs.

If she betrayed the trust the Panthers put in her, they would have retaliated quickly and brutally."

"The police are wrong. I keep telling you and everyone else that, but no one is listening."

"I'm listening." He spoke quietly, knowing that Jenna was more angry about her friend's death than she was about the police investigation or his questions.

"It's just not right, Nikolai. Magdalena lived an upright life. She had a strong faith and a strong sense of justice. Everyone who knew her loved her."

And yet she was dead.

Nikolai didn't say what he was thinking. It wouldn't help, and could only hurt Jenna more than she already had been. "We'll prove that she was the woman you remember."

"I hope so." She rubbed her forehead, and Nikolai could see pain in her eyes.

"Headache?"

"You could say that."

"But you wouldn't?"

"A headache doesn't come close to describing the pain shooting through my head."

"Do you have medicine?"

"The doctor prescribed some, but I haven't taken any yet."

"Where is it?"

"In my purse. In the bedroom." She gestured to a door on the far wall.

"Here," Nikolai said, leading her to the couch. "Lie down. I'll get the medicine and some water."

"You've done enough already. I can manage." But even as she said it, she was settling onto the couch, pulling a throw pillow under her head and closing her eyes.

Nikolai walked into the small bedroom, scanning the room until he spotted Jenna's purse. A small bottle of pills was in the front pocket, and he poured one of the tablets into his hand.

By the time he'd found a glass and filled it with water, Jenna was breathing deeply, her face relaxed in sleep. She looked young and vulnerable, and Nikolai didn't have the heart to wake her. He left the pill on the end table and set the glass beside it. Then he pulled a throw from the back of a chair and draped it over her. She stirred but didn't open her eyes.

It was time to leave, but Nikolai hesitated. There was no security system, no way to protect Jenna from anyone who might decide to break in.

He examined the lock on the door. He could lock it, but the bolt could only be engaged from the inside unless he had a key. Which he didn't.

Maybe he should sleep outside the door just to make sure no one breached Jenna's sanctuary.

And maybe he was too tired to think straight.

The fact was, Jenna was no less safe here than she'd have been at a hotel. As a matter of fact, she was probably safer. There was a house full of people sleeping around her, and a killer would much prefer to attack when his victim was alone.

The thought was cold comfort as Nikolai turned the lock on the door and stepped outside. The sky had lightened, deep black turning to navy blue. Night sounds had ceased, the frogs and insects no longer calling out to each other. In the resulting silence, Nikolai was sure he heard the pad of feet on grass. He slipped into the shadows at the corner of the house, waiting and watching as the minutes ticked by. Another soft sound followed the first, this one coming from behind him. He eased around, his ears straining, his heart pumping adrenaline through him.

A dark shadow appeared, moving toward the door that Nikolai had just exited. He waited, barely breathing as the shadow slid closer. Just a few more steps, a few more heartbeats.

Something jingled, the sound reminding Nikolai of keys

hitting against one another, but he didn't have time to figure out what he was hearing. He lunged forward, tackling the would-be intruder before he could reach Jenna's door.

TWELVE

A loud bang woke Jenna from uneasy sleep. She jerked upright, her heart slamming against her ribs.

"Nikolai?" she called out, but there was no answer.

Another bang followed the first, and this time Jenna was sure she heard a male voice. She rushed for the door, hesitating with her hand on the knob. Had Nikolai gone outside and been attacked?

She'd barely had time to consider the question when the knob turned beneath her hand. Her heart jumped to her throat, and she screamed, the sound more a squeak than a shout.

She pivoted, running to the kitchen. A knife. There had to be a knife in one of the drawers. She opened the first, found nothing. Opened the second and pulled out a butter knife. Not the perfect weapon, but beggars couldn't be choosers.

Please, God, let it be enough.

She whirled back around as the door flew open, her head pounding as her pulse raced.

A man stumbled inside. Dark hair, slim, muscular build. "John?"

"He was skulking around outside your door." Nikolai stepped in behind him, his dark eyes flashing with anger.

"It's my house. I wouldn't call walking around in the backyard skulking." John spat out the response, and Jenna was surprised by the venom in his tone. She'd always thought of him as mild-mannered and slow to irritation, but the stress of Magdalena's death and funeral seemed to be wearing on him.

"It's four in the morning. What reason do you have for *walking* around in your yard?"

"I think the better question would be what reason do *you* have for being in my yard at four in the morning?" John moved farther into the room, the heavy scent of cologne and alcohol sweeping in with him.

"Nikolai was visiting me," Jenna cut in, hoping to ease the building tension.

"I didn't realize the two of you were an item."

"We're not," she said too quickly, heat creeping up her neck and into her cheeks. That was the curse of red hair and fair skin. She could never hide her emotions.

"You're not an item, but he's here in the wee hours of the morning, *visiting*." John frowned, the sarcasm oozing through his voice, then took a deep breath. "Look, that didn't come out the way I meant it to. It's none of my business what you choose to do—"

"We're not *doing* anything."

"As I said, it's none of my business. I just saw the car out front, and I was worried. After everything that's been happening, I wanted to make sure you were okay."

"I appreciate that, John."

"You saw my car out front?" Nikolai speared John with a look that would have sent Jenna running if it had been leveled at her. Just a few minutes ago, he'd stood with his hand on her shoulder, his face soft with compassion. Now, he looked cold and hard, nothing like the man who'd left his house and come running to her side.

"It's parked in front of my driveway. Of course, I saw it."

"It's an early hour to be awake."

"And, yet, here we all are. Wide awake." John smiled, but Jenna didn't miss the heat in his words.

Neither man seemed willing to back down or back off.

Both seemed suspicious of each other. Their tension filled the room, and Jenna's head pounded with renewed vigor.

She should never have called Nikolai. She still wasn't sure why she had. The silence of the house, the darkness pressing in from outside and her own chaotic thoughts had conspired to make her feel vulnerable and alone.

And now she wasn't alone.

She collapsed onto the sofa, her stomach lurching with the sudden movement. "I'm sure we all have too much on our minds to sleep. I'm sorry if Nikolai's car caused you concern, John. I certainly didn't mean to worry you."

John turned his attention from Nikolai and offered Jenna a tight nod. "It's no problem. I just wanted to make sure you were okay. Since you are, I'll go back into the main house."

"Here," Nikolai said, lifting a glass from the side table and handed Jenna a white pill that sat beside it. "Take this. You look pale."

"I'm always pale. It goes with the red hair." She tried to smile, but her hands were shaking. She took the glass, water sloshing onto her pants and the sofa. "Great." She stood quickly, swaying as the pain in her head burst into a kaleidoscope of sparkling lights.

"Slow down, Jen. There's no hurry." Nikolai's hands cupped her upper arms, his warmth seeping into her chilled skin. She could have stood there for hours, could have given in to temptation and leaned her head against his chest, let herself rest there for a while.

Could have, but knew she shouldn't.

She stepped away, her arms still warm from his touch. "I'm fine. It's just these migraines I've been having." She blinked rapidly, hoping the colorful aura would disappear.

"Magdalena had horrible migraines. I have some of her medicine if you need it," John offered, his tension easing as the conversation shifted.

"I have something. Thanks, though." She swallowed the

pill with some water, trying to think past the pounding pain in her head.

"I didn't realize Magdalena suffered from migraines." It was something she'd have thought her friend would have mentioned, but, then, Magdalena had never been one to complain. No matter what was happening in her life, she'd always maintained an upbeat attitude.

"Just since Ben was born. They were brutal. Sometimes she was home in bed for days."

"She never mentioned them."

"You know how she was. She never wanted to admit to weaknesses." John dropped onto the recliner, and Jenna had the impression he planned to stay a while.

"I always thought it was that she wanted to keep a positive attitude, rather than spending time complaining."

"You didn't know her as well as I did." He offered a smile that didn't reach his eyes.

She wanted to argue. She'd known Magdalena longer, after all. But what would be the point? With Magdalena dead, it didn't matter who had known her better or even the reasons why she'd kept her migraines to herself. "Maybe not."

"The thing is," John continued as if she hadn't spoken. "She changed after Benjamin was born. She used to be happy and carefree, but after his birth, she got quiet. It was as if the weight of the world were on her shoulders."

"She seemed happy in Mexico," Jenna said, leaning a hip on the edge of the couch. If she sat down, would John think that she wanted to continue the conversation? Because what she really wanted was for him to leave. There was a vibe about him when he mentioned Magdalena that she didn't like.

"I'm glad. It helps to know that her last few days were pleasant. The police…" His voice trailed off, and he looked away.

"What?"

"They think that Magdalena's migraines might have led to an addiction to narcotics. They think she might have needed money to feed her addiction and agreed to traffic drugs for the Mexican Panthers to pay for it."

"You've got to be kidding me! They can't really think that." Jenna straightened, nearly knocking into Nikolai as she whirled around and paced across the room.

"I thought you should know. Things are starting to come out about Magdalena, and the media may get wind of them. Her death was a pretty big story around here, and people want to know why she died." .

"She died because she was in the wrong place at the wrong time."

"That's what I used to think, but the police think otherwise. I've got to admit, I'm starting to believe them."

"How can you say that, John? She was your wife. She devoted her life to you and your son."

"She devoted her life to her job. To making money. She loved the finer things in life. Look around you. I wanted a spare room for my parents to sleep in. Magdalena insisted we have an entire wing for them. 'Let's show them what we've accomplished. Let's let them know how far we've come.' That's what she said. It was her philosophy of life."

"Her philosophy of life, if you want to call it that, was service to God and to others."

"That's what she wanted the world to think." He shook his head sadly, and Jenna wanted to walk over and knock some sense into him.

"It's the truth. Why else would she have left you and Benjamin and traveled to Mexico a couple times a year?"

"I already told you what the police think."

"I'm not asking what they think. I'm asking what *you* think." Her voice rose, and she was helpless to stop it.

"I think that I didn't know my wife as well as I thought. I think that you didn't know your friend as well as you thought you did."

"Come on, John. That's a cop-out. We both knew her, and we both know that she wasn't capable of what she's being accused of." Jenna tried to rein in her anger, but the throbbing pain in her head seemed to have robbed her of her good sense and self-control.

"Deluding ourselves into believing that an innocent woman was targeted by one of the most notorious drug cartels in Mexico isn't going to give either of us closure. There was a reason Magdalena was murdered. We have to be willing to admit it."

"Admit what? In my opinion, the only people deluded are the police if they think that an upstanding citizen suddenly became a criminal and you if you think that Magdalena's death means you no longer owe her your loyalty."

"I resent that, Jenna. You know I loved Magdalena. It breaks my heart to think—"

"Then don't think it." She nearly shouted and colors flashed in front of her eyes again.

"I think that this conversation might be best continued at another time." Nikolai spoke with quiet authority, his calmness defusing Jenna's anger.

"You're right. I don't think either one of us is thinking clearly right now. I apologize, John. I didn't mean to imply that you didn't love Magdalena."

"I'm sorry, too." He stood, shooting a quick look in Nikolai's direction. Would he have said more if Nikolai hadn't been there? Was there more that Jenna didn't know? Some other reason that John seemed so willing to believe his wife guilty of drug trafficking?

"Did your wife have any enemies, John?" Nikolai asked, the question unexpected. It hung in the air, the silence that followed it almost deafening.

John lifted the glass of water from the side table and carried it into the kitchen. He set it in the sink, and then turned to face Nikolai. "I thought we just agreed that this conversation was better off happening another time."

"I'm not asking if there was a reason why the Mexican Panthers wanted your wife dead. I'm asking if someone else might have. A coworker? Someone she butted heads with or who might have felt threatened by something she knew?"

"Of course not."

"You're sure?" Nikolai pressed, and John's expression tightened, his mouth drawing into a thin line.

"Of course I am."

"That's interesting." Nikolai leaned a shoulder against the wall, his gaze never leaving John's face. What was he thinking? What was he really asking?

"What do you mean, Jansen? Interesting how?"

"You said you weren't sure you knew your wife as well as you'd once thought, but you're sure she had no enemies."

"What's your point?"

"That you either knew your wife and know she didn't have enemies or you didn't and don't."

"I'm not up to word games, so how about you just cut to the chase and tell me what your point is."

"I'm a private investigator. Jenna has asked me to prove that Magdalena is innocent of drug trafficking. To do that, I need to get a feel for who your wife was. I thought you'd be the best place to begin, but you're saying you knew her and that you didn't know her all in the same breath."

"You're investigating my wife's murder?"

"Her life. That's what will help me discover the truth." Nikolai seemed neither apologetic nor defensive, and Jenna found his calm demeanor comforting. Despite John's words, there was no way she'd ever believe that Magdalena was the woman the police were painting her to be. Someone had planted drugs in her bags in Mexico. Someone had planted them in her home. Who? Why? These were questions Jenna was desperate to find answers to.

"Ask me any questions you'd like when the sun is up, Nikolai. Right now, though, I think a few hours of sleep would do me a world of good. I'm sure Jenna could use some rest, too." He walked to the door and opened it, letting cool air drift in.

"I'll stop by tomorrow," Nikolai said, not bothering to ask if that would work. "We can talk then."

"Sounds good. Make it after noon. My parents are going to take Benjamin to the park this morning, and I'm planning to catch up on some sleep while they're gone. The reading of the will is at three, so you'd have to be here before then."

"I'll be here at one." Nikolai smiled, but Jenna saw something in his eyes that made her think he was judging every word John said. Judging and finding him wanting.

"Again, I'm sorry for busting in on you like this, Jenna. As I said, I saw the car and wanted to make sure you were okay. In retrospect, I probably should have picked up the phone and called." John turned his trademark smile on Jenna. That was what had attracted Magdalena to him, and she'd often told Jenna that John's smile was the best thing about him. It left Jenna cold.

"This is your home, and I'm a guest. I should have thought of that before I called Nikolai." She didn't bother explaining that she'd told Nikolai not to come. What would be the point? He had. John had seen his car, and now they were all standing awkwardly in the small foyer of the guest suite.

"You're welcome to have guests over. As a matter of fact, my mother wanted to invite you to dinner after the will is read. Why don't you come along, too, Nikolai?" He glanced at Nikolai who was watching intently.

"I'm sure he has other things to do."

"Actually, I don't."

"Great. I'll see you both tomorrow." John walked out the door and disappeared around the corner of the house.

"I'd better go, too." Nikolai stood in the doorway, his dark eyes skimming over Jenna's face, touching her cheeks, her jaw, her lips before meeting her eyes again. "Will you be okay here by yourself?"

"Of course."

"Is there a door into the main house from inside the guest suite?"

"Yes."

"And there's a lock on that door?"

"A lock and a bolt. Why?"

"You've got the bolt pulled?"

"No. I didn't see any need."

"How about you humor me and go ahead and do it?"

"Sure." She crossed the room, walked down a short hall and locked the door that led into the main house.

"Not very sturdy." Nikolai examined the lock and the bolt, his arm brushing Jenna's as he unlocked the door and then locked it again. "And I suppose that John and his family have a key to get in here."

"I'd imagine so."

"I'm not sure I like this, Jenna. Actually, I'm sure I don't like it."

"That I'm staying here or that I don't have the only key to the lock?"

"Neither makes me happy."

"The only people in the house are John and his family, and I can't see any of them invading my privacy."

"John was wandering around outside your place at four in the morning. Doesn't that strike you as odd?"

"He said he saw your car out front and came to investigate."

"If he wanted to investigate, he could have knocked on this door and checked on you without ever having to leave the house."

"He probably wasn't thinking straight."

"Maybe not."

"You don't like him very much, do you?"

"How I feel about him isn't important. What's important is making sure you're safe here."

"I'm as safe as I'd be anywhere else."

"You'd be safer at my place. Why don't you come back to the apartment with me? You can use my room, and I'll sleep on the couch." He sounded serious, and Jenna could almost imagine going along with his plan. There was no doubt in her mind that she'd be safe there. No doubt that Nikolai would do whatever it took to protect her. Unfortunately, staying at his place when she could barely look him in the eyes without blushing didn't seem like the wisest plan.

"I don't think that's a good idea."

"Why not?"

"Because…"

You're a man and I'm a woman, and I'm not sure that spending the night in the same apartment with you is safe for my heart.

"What?"

"I just don't."

He searched her face as if he could find another answer there.

Finally, he nodded and took a step away. "Keep the doors locked."

"I will."

"And call me if anything comes up."

"It won't."

"I'll be back in a few hours. Try to get some sleep." His knuckles brushed her cheek, leaving a trail of fire before falling away.

Breathless, Jenna stepped back, cool air bathing her cheeks as Nikolai walked outside. "Thanks for coming by, Nikolai. It really meant a lot to me."

"Any time." He smiled, leaned down and pressed a gentle kiss on her forehead. "Now, lock the door and get in bed."

She nodded, her throat tight with a million unspoken words. She wanted to tell him that he'd crossed a line. That kissing her forehead just wasn't something he should have done, but the warmth of his lips lingered on her skin, and she could only close the door and turn the lock.

She flicked off the light and gingerly made her way to the sofa. The medicine she'd taken was beginning to work, the harsh stabbing pain easing to a dull ache. She pulled the comforter over her shoulders, lying down on stiff cushions and closing her eyes.

A few hours of sleep. Both John and Nikolai seemed to think that would solve her woes. They were wrong, of course. Nothing was going to change what had happened. Nothing could ease her sorrow at having lost her best friend.

"Lord, I know You have a reason and purpose for everything, but I don't understand why You allowed Magdalena to be killed. Please, help me find the truth about her death. Help me prove that she really was a wonderful and upright woman." She prayed silently, knowing that God would answer in His own way and His own time. That had been one of the most difficult lessons she'd learned as a Christian. God moved as He would, and though He always answered prayers, those answers were not always what Jenna wanted or expected.

She sighed, punching at the throw pillow, flattening it out to try to ease the last vestiges of her headache. She should get up and go into the bedroom, but her muscles were leaden, her eyes heavy. She closed them, letting the darkness take her.

THIRTEEN

Nikolai glanced at Romero's house as he climbed into the GTO, eyeing the second-story windows, wondering if John's rooms were there. Romero had said he'd seen Nikolai's car and had been worried about Jenna's safety. Nikolai wasn't buying that story.

There was something off about the guy. Something that Nikolai couldn't quite put his finger on. He started the engine, his headlights flashing on a sedan parked at the curb several houses away.

It hadn't been there when he'd arrived and looked similar to the car John had driven to the airport. Curious, he got out of the car and walked to the vehicle. A BMW. All shiny chrome and sleek style. Nikolai placed his hand on the hood and wasn't surprised to find it warm. Someone had parked the car there recently, and he had a feeling he knew who it was.

He jotted the license plate number on a scrap of paper and glanced at his watch. It was early, but the sun would be rising in New York. He suspected that Skylar Grady would be awake with the dawn. Though he'd never met the Information Unlimited employee in person, he'd had several phone conversations with her and had found her both enthusiastic and industrious.

He dialed her number, smiling as Skylar answered on the first ring.

"Skylar, here. What's up?"

"Hey, it's Nikolai."

"Of course it is. Your name is on my caller ID, and that accent is unmistakable. So, I'll ask again. What's up?"

"I'm on a case, and I need some help."

"Cool. I'm all ears."

"I have two names for you. The first is someone who lived in upstate New York during her childhood, so she may be the easiest to track."

"Hold on. Let me grab a pen." The sound of drawers opening and papers rustling filled the phone. "Okay. I'm ready."

"Magdalena Romero. Maiden name, Santiago." He offered the information he'd gleaned from his earlier computer search.

"Jenna's friend?"

"You know her?"

There was a brief pause, and then, "Come on, Jansen. Do you think I'm that out of the loop? Kane has kept me updated on what's been going on. So, what do you want to know?"

"What she was like in high school. What her friends think about her now."

"Got it. Anything else?"

"I need information on her husband, too. The name is John Romero."

"You think he had something to do with Magdalena's death?"

"I think that something isn't right in Houston, and I plan to find out what it is."

"The way I hear it, Magdalena had some serious problems. Drugs were found in her house and in the bags she carried to Mexico. Have you checked into that?"

"The DEA has been investigating."

"And?"

"It sounds like they're convinced that Magdalena was trafficking money and drugs in and out of the country during her trips to Mexico."

"It's not inconceivable. She was a doctor carrying medical

equipment across the border. I doubt the border patrol checked every supply crate. I doubt they'd have checked much of anything she was bringing in. She'd have had an easy time transporting drugs and cash."

"You may be right. The DEA may be right. But Jenna is convinced otherwise, and she's asked me to prove her friend's innocence."

"That's a tall order, Nik."

"Yeah, I know. It doesn't help that the police would be happy to pin the label 'drug trafficker' on Magdalena's gravestone and call it a day."

"Well, you know what they say. If it looks like a skunk and smells like a skunk, it probably *is* a skunk."

"Unless it's a black-and-white cat that was sprayed by a skunk."

"You mean that you think Magdalena was set up?"

"I don't have enough facts to make the call one way or another."

"And the way I hear it, you're playing bodyguard, which is probably limiting your research time. No worries, though. I'll see what I can find out."

"Thanks, Grady."

"No problem." She hung up without saying goodbye. Typical Skylar fashion.

If it looks like a skunk and smells like a skunk…

Skylar's words echoed through his mind as he made the short drive back to his apartment. He'd always been a good judge of character. It was a survival technique he'd learned at a young age and one that had served him well as an adult. People could only hide their true nature for so long. In the end, who they were shone through in what they valued, how they spoke about the people they loved and how they handled adversity.

So far, John Romero wasn't scoring high in any of those areas.

Which meant what?

That the guy was materialistic and self-centered. That he lacked loyalty and compassion. Those things didn't make him a criminal.

But Nikolai still had a bad feeling about the guy.

It edged out any sympathy he had for the loss John had suffered. If he'd truly loved his wife, wouldn't he be shouting her innocence to the world?

Jenna certainly was.

As a matter of fact, she'd been so angered by John's lack of loyalty that Nikolai had wondered if she were going to let him have more than a piece of her mind. If she'd been physically up to the fight, Nikolai would have let the debate rage on. Truth be told, he wouldn't have minded seeing Jenna clobber her arrogant host.

But she *hadn't* been up to it.

If John were any kind of man, he would have seen that and backed off. Instead, he'd argued his point with no concern for Jenna's pale and shaken appearance. It had taken all Nikolai's self-control to keep from doing what he'd wanted to. Taking John out back and beating some sense into him would have felt good, but it wouldn't have accomplished anything except maybe earning him a room in the local jail.

He got out of his car and walked across the parking lot, limping slightly as he made his way up three flights of stairs to his apartment. His bad leg ached from overuse, but he'd rather feel pain than feel nothing. Since he'd nearly lost his foot, that had been a real possibility.

He'd left the curtains open in the living room of his apartment, and gray-blue light spilled in through the sliding-glass door as he walked into the one-bedroom loft. Outside, fingers of gold streaked the horizon, and Nikolai stepped out onto the small terrace, inhaling moist, early-morning air.

He dropped into the vinyl chair and grabbed his Bible from the small glass table beside it. When he was younger and the Jansens' example of faith-filled living had seemed superficial, Nikolai had thought time spent praying and reading the Bible was a waste. The Bible the Jansens presented to him on the day his adoption was finalized had seemed like an inconsequential gift, and he'd shoved it in a drawer and forgotten about it.

Somehow, it had found its way into his things when he'd packed and reported for duty at Marine boot camp. Somehow it had made its way around the world and into every barracks and battlefield. Palm-sized and easy to carry, it had been in his hands more and more as he faced enemy fire and his own mortality.

It had taken a long time, but Nikolai finally understood the example that the Jansens had set. He finally understood the value of taking time out of the day to read God's word and to pray. It was a habit now, and one that often led to clearer thinking and sharper focus.

He opened the Bible, tried to clear his mind, but his thoughts spiraled back to the Romero house. To Jenna leaning against the sofa, her skin as pale and smooth as alabaster, her eyes shadowed with grief and pain and loss. They were things Nikolai understood only too well, and he had wanted to pull her into his arms and tell her that, in time, things would be better.

Concentrating seemed impossible, and he closed his eyes, praying instead. For Jenna and for her friend's family. For himself, that he would find the answers Jenna needed to move forward. He tried to pray for John, as well, but the words fell flat. His heart wasn't in it.

Nikolai scowled, pulling out the scrap of paper he'd written the license plate number on. He had a friend at the DMV who might be willing to access information about the owner of the BMW. If the owner was John, Nikolai would have a few more questions for the man when they met later that afternoon.

In the meantime, he needed to let Kane know what was going on. He dialed the number quickly, not caring that it was still too early to call.

"What's wrong?" Kane's voice was gritty with sleep and filled with a mix of alarm and annoyance.

"You know your sister is staying at the Romero place, right?"

"She called me last night and told me that was plan. Is there a reason why you're calling me in the wee hours of the morning to tell me about it?"

"I don't like the guy."

"Join the crowd. I'm not too fond of him, either. He's slime."

"Did you tell Jenna that?"

"What would be the point? Romero isn't going to ruin her in a day's time. Besides, his parents and son are in the house. It's not like they're alone together."

"That's not what I'm worried about."

"No? Then what's the problem?"

"There's something not right about the guy."

"In what way?"

"He seems way too eager to admit his wife was working with the Mexican Panthers."

"Look, I'm with you in not liking the guy, but as far as the DEA has been able to ascertain, Magdalena was involved in drug trafficking. They've found plenty of evidence pointing to that, and I don't fault Romero for believing it."

"You've spoken to someone with the DEA?"

"Yeah. They've been digging into the family's finances. John has his own bank accounts and savings plans. There's nothing there that doesn't line up with his salary, and the DEA has no reason to believe he's taking payoffs from the Panthers."

"Romero is a defense attorney. He knows how criminals get away with crimes. I'm sure he knows how to hide financial problems if he needs to, and I'm confident he knows exactly how to murder someone and make it look like a random crime."

"Except, Magdalena's death didn't look random. She was specifically targeted by the Panthers. If Romero wanted his wife dead, he could have come up with a lot less troublesome ways to do it."

"You've got a point."

"I should. I've been thinking about it for the better part of two days."

"And you're still comfortable with Jenna staying at the Romero place?"

"It's not my choice one way or another. It's Jenna's decision. But, for the record, I'd say the guy is slime. That doesn't mean he's a criminal."

"It doesn't mean he isn't, either."

"I'm aware of that, too. I want to come back down there, but Maggie is days away from delivering the baby. I need to be here for her and there for Jen, and I'm going crazy worrying about both of them. I'm hoping I can count on you to take the lead on this and make sure Jenna stays safe."

"You know you can. I don't back down from a job once I take it."

"That's why I hired you. So, do me a favor."

"What's that?"

"Get my sister on that plane tomorrow. I won't be happy until she's safe in Washington."

"Will do." Nikolai hung up, no happier than he'd been before he'd called his employer. He trusted Kane's insight but wasn't sure he was right about John Romero.

He glanced at his watch. It was still early. Too early to call the DMV. Too early to call friends and coworkers of the Romeros.

But maybe it wasn't too early to go back to John's house.

It was closing in on six. By the time Nikolai took a shower and made the fifteen-minute drive, he'd be less than two hours early for his breakfast appointment with Jenna.

The way Nikolai saw it, two hours early was just about the right time to show up.

FOURTEEN

Darkness. Silence. Throbbing pain. Jenna tried to open her eyes, but they were sealed shut, the blackness so complete that she knew she was blind again.

She twisted, trying to free herself from the bonds around her wrists and ankles. Twisted again and fell, her eyes flying open as she landed with a thud on the hardwood floor.

Breathless, she scrambled to her feet. She wasn't blind, wasn't bound. The living room of John's guest suite looked exactly the same as it had when he and Nikolai had left.

How long ago had that been?

She glanced at her watch. It was nearly eight, but was it morning or night?

She crossed the room and pulled the curtains open, squinting as bright sunlight streamed into the window. Morning. Of course. She was supposed to attend the reading of the will in a few hours. She'd have dinner with the Romero family after that. Nikolai had mentioned breakfast, but she doubted he'd remember. He was probably home sleeping, resting after a long night of running to Jenna's rescue. Just the thought of her desperate phone call made her blush.

She turned away from the window, freezing when someone knocked on the door. "Yes?"

"Jen? It's Nikolai."

Surprised, she opened the door.

Freshly shaven, his hair damp, Nikolai smelled of mint and

soap and something indefinable, masculine and completely intriguing.

"What are you doing here?"

"We had a breakfast date, remember?"

"A date?"

"Unless you'd like to call it something else."

"How about we just call it breakfast?"

"Whatever works." He glanced around, his gaze settling on the sofa and the blanket that had fallen onto the floor beside it. "Did you just wake up?"

"Yes. I thought you were coming at nine."

"That was the plan."

"But?"

"I figured I'd come over a little early and keep an eye on things."

"You were in the backyard watching the house?"

"I was in the backyard drinking coffee." He held up a thick ceramic mug. "The housekeeper arrived a few minutes after I showed up and offered me some."

"Smells good."

"Want it? I've had plenty." He offered the mug, and Jenna shook her head. Drinking out of the same coffee cup seemed much too intimate.

"No, thanks." She brushed a hand down her flannel pajama bottoms, wishing she'd thought to throw the blanket around her shoulders. Not that Nikolai hadn't already seen her in her pajamas.

"Did anything happen after I left last night?" He settled onto the couch, his dark gaze tracking Jenna's movements as she sat on the arm of the recliner.

"Aside from me falling asleep two seconds after you walked out the door? No."

"You still look tired. Why don't you rest for a while longer?"

"I'll be fine. I just need to take a shower and get dressed. Then we can go."

"I'll wait outside until you're done." He stood, stretching to his full height, his T-shirt pulling tight against taut abs. Not gym muscles, real muscles. The kind guys earned by working hard and playing harder.

The kind any woman would find distracting.

The kind Jenna really shouldn't be staring at.

She blushed, turning her back to Nikolai and pretending to wipe dust from the spotless sofa table. "Maybe this isn't a good idea."

"Sure it is. We both need to eat." He spoke matter-of-factly as he walked to the door.

"I just don't want either of us to get any ideas."

"About what?"

"You. Me. Breakfast dates."

"So you're thinking we may go on more than one?" He smiled, and Jenna's face heated again.

"I don't believe in playing games, Nikolai."

"Neither do I."

"Good, because I've been down this road before. Meeting someone, falling for him—"

"You're saying you're falling for me?" He raised a dark brow, and Jenna scrambled to backtrack.

"I'm saying that I don't *want* to fall for you, and I'm not going to and you need to know that up front."

"All right." He put his hand on the doorknob, ready, it seemed, to end the conversation.

And Jenna should have been ready to end it, too.

Should have been.

"That's it? Just, 'all right'?"

"Should I say something more?"

"I guess not." Although, she'd thought he would.

"Then how about you get ready, we'll go to breakfast as we planned, and we'll let things play out the way they will?"

"Just as long as we understand each other," she mumbled as she hurried into the bedroom, shut the door and pressed her hot forehead to it. What had she been thinking, talking to Nikolai like that? It wasn't as if he'd given any indication that he was pursuing her.

She heard the door open and close and knew Nikolai had walked outside. Relieved, she grabbed some clothes and went into the bathroom, glancing in the mirror and frowning at her reflection. She looked too pale, her hair garishly red, her pajamas hanging from her too-skinny frame.

And she'd stood bold as brass in front of Nikolai and told him that she had no intention of falling for him.

He'd probably been horrified by the idea that she might; relieved that she didn't plan to. He certainly wouldn't have been looking at the woman Jenna saw in the mirror, thinking that he wished she'd fall into his arms.

She showered and dressed quickly, slid her feet into sneakers and opened the door. The morning was bright, the sun splashing down onto the lush green lawn. She took a deep breath of the cool spring air, glancing around, but not seeing Nikolai. Had he gone around to the front of the house?

"Jenna! We're over here," a voice called out, but it wasn't Nikolai's. She turned and spotted John walking around the side of the house, Nikolai by his side.

"Are we all going to breakfast together?" As irritated as she'd been with John the previous night, it might be good to have him around. Anything to distract her from looking too deeply into Nikolai's eyes.

"I wish I could, but I'm spending some time with Ben this morning."

"I thought your parents were taking him to the park," Nikolai said, and John stiffened.

"I don't know what your problem is, Jansen, but I really wish you'd stop trying to catch me in a lie."

"You did say your parents were taking Ben to the park," Jenna cut in, hoping to head off an argument.

"They planned to, but he woke up crying for Magdalena this morning. We felt it would better if I went along with everyone else."

"I'm glad you're going to spend time with him. He really needs you right now." Despite knowing that John loved his son, Jenna hadn't seen him spending much time with Benjamin during the past few days. She'd chalked it up to grief and stress, and it seemed she'd been right. Now that the funeral was over, John seemed more in tune with his son's needs.

"I know. He's only three, and he just doesn't get that his mother isn't coming back. I'll bet he'd love to spend some time with you. A woman close to Magdalena's age might be just the thing he needs to cheer him up. Would you like to come to the park with us?"

"Nikolai and I are going out to breakfast."

"Come when you're done, if you'd like. It's not far from here. Just three blocks north."

"All right."

"Why don't I drive you there when we're finished? I wanted a few minutes to talk to John, anyway. You don't mind, do you, John?" Nikolai asked, but Jenna was sure he had every intention of going to the park and asking the questions whether John agreed or not.

"Sure. We can all come back to the house together when we're done. Magdalena's lawyer will be here at three to read the will and several of her friends will be showing up early for that."

"It's still so hard to believe she's gone." Jenna spoke quietly, the words barely carrying through the quiet morning air.

"I don't think I do believe it. Maybe in a few more days or a few weeks when she doesn't come walking through the door, I'll finally believe she's not coming home."

"It's hard to get used to a world without someone you love in it." For once, Nikolai sounded like he sympathized with John.

"That's for sure." John offered a smile that was barely there before it was gone. "I'd better get back in the house. Benjamin will wonder where I am."

"I'll see you in a couple of hours," Jenna called out as he

turned away, and he waved before disappearing around the side of the house.

"Ready?" Nikolai pressed a hand to Jenna's lower back, urging her toward the front of the house.

"Maybe I should stay and see if there's something I can do to comfort Ben."

"Does he know you well?"

"Not really. We've only seen each other a handful of times."

"Then it might be disconcerting for him to have you there."

"What do you mean?"

"To a little boy who is looking for his mother, another woman might seem like a replacement. I would have said the same to Romero, but I doubted he'd want to hear my advice."

"Maybe not, but I think you're probably right. I just really wish there was some way I could help."

"The best way you can help is to let Ben's family meet his needs. I know it's difficult to do. You loved your friend, and you want to comfort her child, but in the end, only his family can replace the love and stability that have suddenly vanished from his life."

"You sound like you've been in a similar position."

"I've lost friends, if that's what you mean." He opened his car door, waiting as she slid into the passenger seat.

"More than one?"

"I'm a Marine. Not all of my comrades made it home from the war. Some of them had wives and kids. All of them had family."

"I'm sorry." She looked into his eyes, saw a sadness that didn't show on his face, and reached to touch his hand.

"Me, too, but death is a fact of life, and we'd be fools to think that it would never touch us." He turned his hand, capturing hers, his thumb running along the inside of her wrist. Heat shot up her arm, and her pulse jumped.

And she was a teenager again, feeling that first quick leap of chemistry, the first realization that she was growing up and changing and wanting more than she'd ever wanted before.

She tugged her hand from Nikolai's, grabbed the door handle and started to pull it closed.

He put his hand on the window, stopping its momentum. "Does what you feel scare you, Jenna?"

"What are you talking about?"

"I thought you didn't play games."

"I don't."

He nodded, releasing the door, letting her pull it closed.

Letting her stew in her own juices.

A good tactic, but one Jenna didn't much appreciate at the moment.

He slid into the car, not saying a word as he pulled away from the Romero home.

A minute passed, then five, neither of them speaking, until finally Jenna couldn't take the silence any longer. "I'm not playing games, Nikolai."

"I don't think I said you were."

"You implied it."

"I implied that you weren't being honest about how you feel. If that's game playing to you, then maybe it is what you're doing."

"How I feel about what? You?"

"That was the direction of the conversation, so, yes." His accent had thickened, and Jenna could almost imagine him as a young teen in a new country, his native language adding color and depth to the new language he was learning.

"We just met."

"What does length of time have to do with anything?"

"It seems as if it should."

"You don't believe in love at first sight?"

"The first time I saw you, I didn't actually *see* you. And, no, I don't believe in love at first sight."

"Then chemistry, connection, attraction?" He pulled into

the parking lot of a busy diner, parking the car in a space near the front of the building.

"Those things are fleeting, Nikolai. They don't last."

"Not always."

But sometimes they did. He didn't say it, but the idea was there, the thought hanging in the air between them. Maybe this time it would. Maybe this time, chemistry, connection and attraction would lead to something deeper and more lasting.

"I've been in love before. It didn't work out. I'm not sure I ever want to go there again."

"Funny," he said, eyeing her with an intensity that made her squirm.

"What?"

"I didn't take you for a quitter."

"I'm not."

"Then why are you throwing in the towel after one bad experience?"

"I'm…" She was going to say *not* again, but, of course, she was.

"Look, I'm not saying that we're going to fall madly in love, get married, have kids and grow old together." He didn't even look away as he said those things. "I'm just saying that we're here together, and I don't see any reason not to explore what we feel."

"Generally, what I feel when we're together is terror. Because, generally, when we're together, someone is trying to kill me, and you're saving my life."

He laughed, the sound rumbling out into the car as he opened the door.

"You can laugh all you want, but I don't think it's a good time for us to be *exploring* anything."

"If we wait for the right time to do things, we'll sit twiddling our thumbs as life passes us by. Speaking of which, I don't know about you, but I'm hungry." He closed the door and was around the car before Jenna had time to think of a response.

It was probably for the best.

The fact was, she'd never been one to sit around waiting for things to happen. When she'd wanted something, she'd gone after it. Whether that was a trophy at a gymnastics meet or a grade in school, she'd pursued it with zeal. When she'd met Ryan, she'd pursued their relationship the same way, planning and plotting how their future would play out.

And then the doctor had diagnosed her with leukemia, and she'd realized that all those plans were going to fall apart. That everything she'd been working for was worth nothing if she didn't have her health and her life.

"You've gone quiet on me," Nikolai said as they walked across the parking lot.

"Just thinking."

"About?"

"About what you said. Life passing us by while we twiddle our thumbs waiting. I've never done that. Sat around twiddling my thumbs, I mean."

"I didn't think you were the type who would."

"I believe in going after what I want, but I've learned that sometimes the things we want just aren't meant to be."

"That doesn't mean we shouldn't keep trying to find out what *is* meant to be."

"*We're* not. Meant to be, I mean."

"Okay."

"And that's it, again?"

"We both said what we needed to, right?" He smiled, holding open the diner door so that Jenna could walk in.

The scent of bacon and maple syrup hung in the air, and her stomach growled loudly in response. A good meal, a few minutes away from the Romero's house—that's all she needed to clear her head.

And she'd *better* clear it.

Otherwise, she might begin to think too deeply about what Nikolai had said. She might begin to study him more intently, spend more time mentally listing the things about him that she admired.

And then she might find that attraction and chemistry really were turning into something deep and lasting. Something that she'd once wanted but had given up on.

Throwing in the towel was what Nikolai had called it.

Jenna preferred to think of it as self-preservation.

Although, when Nikolai handed her a menu, his eyes dancing with humor and dark with interest, she was tempted to call it cowardice. Ryan, after all, had been a boy when she'd met him. Nikolai was a man, and Jenna had a feeling her heart would do more than break if she let herself fall for him and then had to watch him walk away.

No, Nikolai wouldn't just break her heart.

He'd shatter it, and if he did, Jenna doubted it would ever be whole again.

FIFTEEN

Jenna dug into her pancakes, eggs, hash browns and sausage with gusto, and Nikolai couldn't help smiling as he watched.

"What?" She frowned as she wiped her mouth and set the napkin in her lap, ladylike but for the huge plate of food sitting in front of her. Then again, Nikolai had never thought that picking at food and limiting calories was a ladylike thing to do. For his part, he preferred to eat meals with people who were more interested in enjoying the conversation and the food than in counting every bite.

"Just wondering where you're going to put all that."

"I'll find a place for it." She grinned as she forked a bite of pancake into her mouth.

"I can order you more, if you'd like."

"Sorry. My days of consuming as much as a lumberjack ended around the time I had to give up gymnastics."

"You were a gymnast?"

"From the time I was three until I got sick my senior year of college. I've got boxes filled with trophies and medals. I used to imagine pulling out the boxes and letting my daughters and sons play with them. It's probably long past time to toss them all out." She shrugged, pushing a piece of sausage to the side of her plate.

"Do you no longer want to share them with your children?"

"I can't have kids. That's another thing that cancer stole from me." She said it matter-of-factly, as if she'd practiced the words over and over until they no longer hurt.

"There are other ways of creating a family, Jenna."

"I know. Believe me, I've thought about that plenty. But…"

"What?"

"I always wonder if it would be fair to tell a guy that we can't have biological children together. I know it sounds stupid, but it's how I feel."

"It doesn't sound stupid. It sounds safe."

"What do you mean?" She lifted another bite of pancake, but didn't eat it.

"I mean that you've been in love before and it didn't work out. It's much easier to say that you don't want to disappoint a potential husband than to admit that you're afraid of being disappointed."

Her eyes widened. She opened her mouth, closed it again.

Nikolai was sure she'd tell him that he didn't know what he was talking about.

Instead, she set her fork down, watching him through narrowed eyes. "You're something else, Nikolai."

"Is that a good thing or a bad thing?"

"I haven't decided yet." She paused, cocking her head to the side. "Or maybe I have."

"Yeah?"

"I think it's a good thing that you didn't say what everyone else has. I'm tired of the sympathy and the words of encouragement. I'd rather just be told to get over my pity trip and get on with my life."

"Was that what I said?"

"In your own sweet way."

"Sweet?" He'd been called a lot of things, but never that.

"Would you rather I'd said tough, masculine and forceful?"

"Actually, yes." He smiled over his coffee cup, glad to see Jenna relaxed for a change. She'd been wound up tight since he'd met her, and a few minutes thinking about something other than her friend's death could only be good for her.

"I'll keep that in mind." She shoved her half-full plate toward the center of the table.

"Done?"

"I guess I really didn't have room for all that food. Too bad. It was delicious."

"We can come back tomorrow morning before I take you to the airport and you can have more."

"Actually, John is going to give me a ride to the airport."

"He'd be better off spending that time with his son."

"You're pretty judgmental of him."

"I told you last night that I didn't like him much, but that wasn't quite true."

"No?"

"It isn't that I don't like him much, it's that I don't like him at all."

"That's harsh, Nikolai."

"Maybe, but I have no respect for a man without loyalty."

"I don't think—"

"Does he seem grief-stricken to you, Jenna? Does he seem like a man who has just lost his wife?"

"We can't judge him as callous just because he didn't cry at Magdalena's funeral."

"So, you did notice."

"He has a little boy to think about. It's not as if he can just fall apart."

"I'm surprised you're defending him. Last night, you looked ready to take his head off."

"Magdalena loved him. He can't be all bad."

"No, but I think he has a lot of secrets."

"What do you mean?"

"Remember how I left the guest suite and ran into him outside?"

"How could I forget? The two of you nearly gave me a heart attack."

"He didn't just look out a window and see my car. He was out last night. I don't know where he was. I don't know what he was doing, but his car was parked a few houses up and the engine was still warm."

"Are you sure it was his car?"

"I have a friend who works at the DMV. He looked up the license plate number for me."

"So, he was out. Maybe he couldn't sleep and went for a drive."

"That's the explanation he gave me while I was waiting for you to get ready to come to breakfast."

"But?"

"I'd like to know why he didn't mention being out when we ran into each other last night. I'd also like to know why he didn't ask me to move my car so he could pull up the driveway and into his garage."

"There was a lot going on. He may simply have for-got-en."

"Maybe."

"But you don't think he did?"

"I think he was hoping I wouldn't notice his car. I think he'd have preferred it if neither of us knew he was out last night."

"What he does is his business, so I'm not sure why he would care."

"He wouldn't. Unless he had something to hide."

"Like what?" She sighed, rubbing the back of her neck, her frustration obvious. Whether she was frustrated by Nikolai's comments, by her own doubts about John, or by all the unanswered questions, Nikolai didn't know.

"That's what I want to find out."

"I thought you were looking into Magdalena's life. Not her husband's."

"Aren't they one and the same?"

"Not really. Magdalena had a career and outside interests that didn't include John. He had his own interests as well."

"Like what?"

"The humanitarian medical missions were all Magdalena's thing. John never traveled with her, even before they had Ben."

"Did that cause problems between them?"

"I think Magdalena would have liked John to participate, but she wasn't angry about it. There were never fights or arguments about whether or not he would go. And it wasn't that he didn't take an interest. He did small things, like arranging for the medical supplies to be shipped and unloaded."

"So, Magdalena was mostly interested in charity. What about John? What things did he enjoy?"

"Fishing. Football. Hunting. He had a lot of hobbies. As a matter of fact, the last time I visited, I didn't even see him."

"Didn't you think that was odd?"

"Not really. I was only in town for a couple of days."

"How long ago was that?"

"A little over two years. I'd just found out my cancer was in remission and I flew out here to visit."

"Yeah?" He kept his comment vague, not wanting to stop the flow of Jenna's words. She had plenty of memories of Magdalena and John. Some of those memories might help Nikolai get a clearer picture of who the couple was and where they'd gone wrong.

And he had no doubt they had gone wrong.

A couple that spent more time apart than together didn't seem like a couple destined to last. Perhaps that explained why John hadn't seemed grief-stricken over his wife's death. It might also explain why he'd been out until nearly four in the morning.

"They lived in the condo, then. It was maybe a third of the size of what they have now. It was comfortable, but nothing fancy."

"Was there a reason for the move?"

"Are you interrogating me, Nikolai?" she asked, spearing him with a hard look as the waitress took their plates and handed Nikolai the check.

"I'm asking questions that I hope will help me understand Magdalena and John."

"Speaking of John, we'd probably better head to the park if we're going to meet his family there." She stood and stretched, her T-shirt riding up to reveal a sliver of pale smooth flesh. She tugged it back into place as she leaned over to pull the check from his hand. "I've got this."

"I don't think so." He pulled it back, calling the waitress over and handing her cash.

"I wish you hadn't done that," Jenna mumbled as the waitress walked away.

"Why?"

"Because this wasn't a date. It was just two people having breakfast together, so I should have paid my own way."

"You can pay next time."

"I'm leaving tomorrow morning. I don't think there'll be time for another meal together."

"We're stopping here on the way to the airport, remember?"

"John is driving me, *remember?*" she asked, smiling.

"You're going to deny me that pleasure of escorting you back to the airport?"

"I'm sure you have better things to do with your time."

"Like?"

"Like whatever private investigators do."

"I'm not just a private investigator. I'm a man who would like the pleasure of your company one more time before you go back to Washington. Seeing as how I've saved your life twice, I don't think that's too much to ask."

"You saved my life three times, but I thought we weren't counting."

"We're not, unless counting means I get my way."

She laughed, the sound soft and filled with amusement.

"Fine. If it's that important to you, I guess I can't say no."

But she could have, and they both knew it. Just as they both knew there was something simmering beneath the surface of everything they said, every glance they exchanged.

"What time does your plane leave?"

"Ten."

"I'll pick you up at seven."

Jenna walked out of the diner ahead of Nikolai, her hair gleaming in the bright sunlight. He wanted to put an arm around her shoulders and let his fingers play in the silky ends of her hair. He wanted to forget about John Romero and his poor deceased wife and enjoy the time he was spending with Jenna. He couldn't, though, because forgetting those things could make him forget the danger that Jenna might still be in, and that could prove hazardous for both of them.

His car was parked just a few yards away, and Nikolai followed Jenna as she stepped off the curb. An engine revved to their left, and he turned, saw a motorcycle pull out of a space a few feet away. There were several other motorcycles dotting the parking lot, and the driver seemed no more aware of Nikolai than he should be. Still, Nikolai tensed, edging Jenna back toward the curb.

"What's wrong?" she asked, but Nikolai kept his eyes on the approaching motorcycle, wishing he still had his service weapon. Wishing he had any weapon. A gun. A knife. A pitchfork. Whatever would work to keep Jenna safe.

The motorcycle sped closer, the engine revving again, and Nikolai pushed Jenna between two cars, ignoring her scream as he turned to face the oncoming vehicle. There was no way he could stop the attack. No way he could keep the motorcyclist from doing whatever he planned.

"Stay down!" he shouted, praying the driver didn't have a gun. Praying that Jenna would do as he'd ordered.

But of course she didn't.

She was up and moving toward him as the motorcycle

swerved. The driver lifted something dark and familiar. Not a gun. A hand grenade?

"Move!" He dove between the cars, lifting Jenna and running, the motorcycle's engine filling the morning air, his heart beating loudly in his ears.

And for a moment he was back in Iraq, the morning stillness broken by an explosion, adrenaline pumping. Anger and fear and determination all rolling through him, rolling over him until he couldn't tell one from another. Didn't know anything but his own need to protect and to survive.

He yanked Jenna around the side of the building, pressing her against the brick wall, hoping it would be enough to keep her safe. The sound of the motorcycle faded. The morning stillness returned.

"Is he gone?" Jenna gasped the words, her face so pale Nikolai thought she might pass out.

"Yes."

"He had something in his hand. Did you see it? It looked like—"

"It looked like a hand grenade. That's what it looked like, but it was a dud. Otherwise it would have exploded. Come on. We'd better see if it's lying on the ground somewhere." He took her hand, leading her back the way they'd come, scanning the ground.

"Did he actually throw it?" Jenna asked, more strength in her voice than there'd been a moment ago.

"I don't know. I was too busy running to pay much attention."

"He looked like he was going to."

"You wouldn't know that if you'd done what I'd said and stayed back." He got down on his belly, peering beneath the cars, his blood freezing when he spotted what he was looking for. "Do you have a cell phone?"

"Yes."

"Call 911."

"Is it under there?" She moved closer, and Nikolai shot her a look he hoped would freeze her in place.

He should have known better.

She eased onto her stomach, looked under the car, her hair brushing his arm as she angled to get a better look. He caught a whiff of vanilla and maple syrup, felt the warmth of her shoulder pressing against his, heard her deep inhalation as she saw what he had.

"It really *is* a grenade. Should we get it out from under there?"

"That depends on whether we want to go home in my car or in body bags."

"I guess that means no."

"We can't know if there are explosives in it, and we can't know if the next movement will set it off. Call 911. I'm going to make sure the owner of this car doesn't come out of the diner and run over the grenade." He scooted forward on his belly, trying to get a better look. It looked Army issue and old, but he couldn't see enough details to say for sure. What he could see was that the pin had been removed. The person who'd tossed it had meant to do serious harm. By the grace of God, he hadn't been successful.

Jenna's voice spilled into his thoughts, her frantic words barely registering as Nikolai stood and paced the length of the car. Just the night before, Officer Daniels had said that Jenna was no longer being targeted by the Panthers. Either he'd been wrong or someone else was determined to do her harm.

Who?

Why?

Nikolai didn't know, but he did know that Jenna hadn't survived the Panthers' stronghold to die on the streets of Houston. He believed that as firmly as he believed it was his job, maybe even his duty to make sure whoever was coming after her was caught and that that person paid the price.

SIXTEEN

"There's a grenade under a car!" Jenna shouted into the phone, repeating the words for what seemed like the hundredth time.

"You're saying someone threw a grenade at you and it rolled under a car, and you need the police?" the operator asked, her tone reflecting her disbelief.

"That is exactly what I'm saying."

"Tell her the pin has been pulled out of the grenade." Nikolai's voice was calm, and he seemed completely comfortable with the idea that they were standing just a few feet away from a live grenade.

Jenna was not.

She relayed the information to the operator, her pulse pounding behind her eyes, the headache that never seemed far away, rearing up again.

A police car sped into the parking lot, lights flashing, sirens blaring. The door swung open and an officer jumped out, his salt-and-pepper hair and lined face giving him a kind and comforting appearance.

"I'm Officer Desmond. Is there a problem here, folks?"

"We explained the situation to the 911 operator." Nikolai walked toward him, and the officer nodded.

"A grenade under a car, right?"

"That's right."

"You're sure? Those things aren't so easy to get your hands on."

"I was in the Marines for years. I've seen my fair share of them. It looks old. Maybe from World War II."

"That's a possibility. I've seen them being sold as collectibles. Of course, none of them are live. Where is it?"

"It's here. Behind the back left tire of the car." Nikolai gestured to a beat-up Toyota, and the officer dropped down onto his hands and knees and peered beneath the car.

"You're right. Looks like we've got ourselves a grenade. Won't know if it has explosives in it until we attempt a detonation." The officer stood, his green eyes settling on Jenna. Did she look as sick as she felt? As terrified?

"Does Houston have a bomb squad?" Nikolai asked, and the officer nodded.

"They've already been notified. Should be here any minute. In the meantime, I'm going to start clearing out the diner. If this thing does have explosives in it and it goes off, the car'll explode. That could take out a huge chunk of the parking lot and the building." He opened the trunk of his cruiser and pulled out crime scene tape, cordoning off the area surrounding the grenade and shooing away the small crowd of people who'd begun to gather.

"You folks can wait across the street, too," he said as he finished with the crime scene tape. "Don't disappear, though. We'll have some questions for you once we get things under control."

Jenna nodded, then wished she hadn't. Lights exploded in front of her eyes, and her stomach heaved. She was going to be sick. Really sick. Right there in the parking lot of the diner with Nikolai, Officer Desmond and a small crowd of people looking on.

She put a hand out, felt warm muscle beneath soft knit, and realized that she'd closed her eyes, was reaching blindly. She opened them, looked into Nikolai's deep brown eyes. Her hand rested against his chest, her fingers curving into the soft fabric of his shirt. "Sorry."

She tried to pull away, but he pressed her hand closer, his palm rough and calloused, his heartbeat a subtle vibration beneath her hand. He was nervous, too. She could feel it in his taut muscles and rapid pulse, but it didn't show on his face.

"It's okay," he said, his voice rumbling out, deep and soothing as he wrapped his free arm around her waist, pulled her close so that their hands were sandwiched between their bodies.

She could have stepped back easily. His hold was that light, his touch that tentative. Instead, she moved even closer, her hand slipping from beneath his, her arms wrapping around his waist. Firm muscles and warm skin and a solid presence that she couldn't help but hold onto.

She took a steadying breath, inhaling mint and masculinity before she eased away from Nikolai. Her stomach pitched again, but she ignored that, and the pain that was rocketing through her head.

"We'd better move back and give the police some room to work." Her voice sounded dull and lifeless, but at least she was talking, moving, thinking.

They walked across the lot, merging into the crowd that had formed across the street. Excited voices, whispered speculations and high-pitched exclamations rose above the sound of sirens and shouted orders to stay back.

"Ma'am? Sir?" A tall, well-built police officer approached, his eyes as black as pitch, his skin deeply tanned.

"I'm Sergeant Anderson. I'd like to ask you a few questions. Would you mind coming with me?" He turned before they could respond, leading them away from the crowd and to a dark SUV parked on the street. They were nearly a half block away from the diner, but Jenna could clearly see the bomb squad van and half a dozen police cars that had converged on the parking lot.

Sergeant Anderson opened the back door of the SUV and

motioned for Jenna to climb in. "We can talk here or down at the station. Whichever is more comfortable for you."

"Here is fine," she responded without giving it much thought. What did it matter where they answered his questions? The results would be the same. There was no way the police were going to be able to find the guy on the motorcycle. Jenna had barely had time to see him before he'd lobbed the grenade. What little she had to offer by way of information would give the police absolutely nothing to go on.

She got in the backseat of the SUV, scooting over as Nikolai climbed in beside her.

"Can I have both of your names?" the sergeant asked, glancing up from a notebook he was writing in.

"Jenna Dougherty," Jenna responded, and he paused, frowning.

"Have you had contact with the Houston Police Department recently?"

"Someone attempted to shoot her yesterday. He was taken into custody yesterday afternoon." Nikolai offered the information, and Sergeant Anderson nodded.

"I remember hearing about the case. It's connected to the Mexican Panthers, right?"

"That's what we're being told."

"Who's the officer in charge?"

"Daniels."

"He's in narcotics. I'll give him a call. You two wait here, and we'll finish the interview when I'm done." It sounded more like an order than a suggestion, and Jenna had the feeling she'd been downgraded from victim to suspect in the time it took for her to say her name.

Sergeant Anderson took a few steps away, turning so that his back was to Jenna and Nikolai as he spoke on the phone.

"Why do I suddenly feel like a criminal?" she asked.

"Guilt by association, I guess. You were friends with a woman the DEA is investigating. You were with her in Mexico when she was abducted and killed. The Mexican Panthers are pursuing you."

"Apparently, so are the police and the DEA. I need to call my brother. See if he's heard anything about a search warrant on my house." She pulled out her cell phone, but Nikolai gestured toward Sergeant Anderson.

"You may want to wait. It looks like Anderson is coming back. I have a feeling he'll be able to tell you everything you want to know about the search warrant."

He'd barely finished speaking when the door opened and Sergeant Anderson got in the SUV. He shifted so that he was facing Jenna, and he didn't look happy. "I spoke to Officer Daniels. He'll be here in fifteen minutes. We also have some DEA and FBI agents coming over. We need to trace how the hand grenade made its way to Houston, and we need to find out who was carrying it. If you wouldn't mind waiting outside of the car, Mr. Jansen, I'll interview you one at a time and see if either of you have information that can help the investigation."

"Are you up to being questioned, Jenna?" Nikolai asked, as if Jenna actually had a choice in the matter.

"It's now or later, so I guess it may as well be now." She tried to smile but failed miserably.

"I'll be right outside if you need me." He got out, shooting a quick, hard glance in Sergeant Anderson's direction. No doubt there was an unspoken message in it. Some warning about not pushing too hard or asking too much.

Or maybe not.

As much as Nikolai seemed determined to protect Jenna, he treated her like she was perfectly capable of protecting herself. There was no fawning over or pandering to her, and she appreciated that. She'd spent two years of her life looking into the eyes of people who pitied her. She'd spent that same amount of time trying to maintain her independence and prove to her friends and family that she was still the strong, tough person she'd been before her diagnosis.

"Ms. Dougherty? Are you ready?" Sergeant Anderson asked, and Jenna blinked. Had he asked the question before?

She didn't know, and her face heated. "I'm sorry. It's been a long few days, and I'm not quite myself."

"You've been under a lot of stress since your friend's death. Magdalena Romero was her name, right?"

"That's right."

"I'm sorry for your loss. I lost a close friend a year ago, and I know how difficult it is to say goodbye." He spoke quietly, and Jenna didn't doubt the sincerity in his gaze.

"Thank you."

"I also understand that a lot of things have been happening since your return from Mexico. Things that are completely out of your control. Whatever you've done, Jenna, you don't deserve to die for it." He said it so calmly, Jenna almost missed the point. When she got it, really got it, she straightened in her seat and leaned toward him.

"What do you mean? What do you think I've done?"

"It's not what I think. It's what the narcotics unit thinks. You know they've just obtained a search warrant to enter your home in Washington, right? What do you think they'll find when they search it?"

"An old tomcat, and a couple of bags of mini–chocolate bars. There may also be a dead mouse. I was feeding one who lived in the wall, but Dante—my cat—wasn't too fond of that, and he may have dispatched the poor little thing while I was gone."

"This isn't a time for jokes, Jenna."

"You asked what they'd find. I'm telling you."

"If they find something else, then you're going to be in some very serious trouble."

"You mean like a stockpile of drugs or weapons or cash? Do I look like the sort of person who'd get involved in that stuff?"

"You'd be surprised at what the average drug runner looks like."

"I've been to Mexico one time. You know that, right? It would be a little difficult for me to be a master drug trafficker when I never go anywhere."

"I only know what I've been told. The DEA is investigating you and your friend. There's been an influx of drugs into Texas border towns over the past four or five years. That coincides with the timing of your friend's first mission trip to Mexico."

"That's circumstantial."

"It's compelling when you consider that she was executed by one of the most notorious drug cartels in Mexico. Compelling when you know that drugs were found with her belongings and in her home."

"I—" But what could she say that she hadn't said before? "I thought you were going to question me about the guy who tossed the hand grenade."

"I will. I just wanted things to be clear between us before we began. By the time the DEA arrives, your house will have been searched. Whatever is there will be in their hands. If you're up front with me now, maybe we can strike a deal with the prosecutor—"

"Are you arresting me?"

"That isn't what I said."

"You're talking about a prosecuting attorney and plea bargaining."

"In the event that something is found in your house—"

"Nothing will be."

"Then you have nothing to worry about. Now, how about you tell me about the guy who threw the hand grenade?" And as quickly as that, he changed the subject.

Jenna should have been relieved, but she wasn't. Someone had framed Magdalena and made it seem as if a loving, compassionate woman was a coldhearted criminal. Jenna didn't know why or how, but she knew it had happened, and if it had happened to Magdalena, it could happen to her.

Fear coursed through her, adding to the pounding pain in her head and the roiling nausea in her gut. She needed cool, fresh Washington air to clear her head. She needed the sweet little cottage on the edge of the Centennial Trail that she'd bought a year ago. She needed her church family and her brother and his wife and son.

And maybe, just maybe, she needed Nikolai to get back in the car and play macho protector while she did what she wanted to and let all her fear and sadness and anger overflow into a waterfall of tears.

SEVENTEEN

One hour and twenty-seven minutes.

That's how long it took the Houston Bomb Squad to safely detonate the hand grenade. Not that Nikolai would have wanted them to rush things. He'd have been happy to sit in the back of the SUV for several more hours if not for the fact that Jenna was sitting beside him, pale and shaken and much too quiet.

"It looks like everything is clear," Sergeant Anderson said, opening the back door and motioning for Nikolai and Jenna to get out. "I appreciate your cooperation in this matter. Sorry for making you wait for so long. I think Officer Daniels has a few questions for you, and then you'll be free to go."

"I've got a few questions for Daniels, too," Nikolai responded.

"I'm sure he'll be happy to answer them." Anderson led the way across the parking lot and through a throng of people hovering just behind yellow crime scene tape.

"How much longer do you think this will take?" Jenna asked, her voice quiet and sedate as if she'd used up all her energy hours ago.

Concerned, Nikolai stopped, turning to face her. "If this is too much for you, we can put it off for a few hours."

"There's no sense in that. One way or another, I'm going to have to face Officer Daniels and the DEA and any other law enforcement entity that decides it wants to throw charges at me."

"Who said anything about charges?"

"The only other person I've spoken to in the past hour and a half." She gestured at Anderson's back, her eyes flashing with a mix of irritation and worry.

"I didn't say that charges would be pressed against you, Jenna," Anderson said. "I simply let you know that the DEA was investigating to see if you were involved in Dr. Romero's drug trafficking scheme." The officer didn't glance over his shoulder as he spoke, and he didn't stop walking. Apparently, he was as anxious to get rid of them as they were to get rid of him.

"Now it's a scheme?" Jenna's voice rose, and a hint of color tinged her cheeks.

"How about you ask Officer Daniels that question? I'm not privy to all the information he has regarding the case."

"What case? My friend is dead and the entire police department seems content to let her murder go unpunished."

"What we're trying to do is find out the truth about her death." To his credit, Anderson seemed unfazed by Jenna's comment, and at his calm response, the color in her cheeks deepened.

"I know you work hard to protect the people of this community, and I know that you do the best you can to find criminals and put them in jail. The thing is, my friend isn't a criminal. Neither am I."

"I'd like to believe you, Jenna. Unfortunately, most of the people who tell me that they're innocent, aren't. Most of the family members and friends of those people have no idea about the kind of criminal activity they're involved in. Hey! Daniels! Over here," he called out, and Officer Daniels stepped away from a small group of men and women.

Daniels smiled as he approached, offering Nikolai and Jenna brief handshakes. "I'm sorry for keeping you folks here for so long."

"You wanted to ask us a few questions?" Jenna brushed thick bangs from her forehead, her hand trembling. She looked scared to death, and Nikolai moved closer, dropping a hand to her shoulder and offering support in the only way he could.

"Yes, and I'm sure we're all anxious to get on with our days, so I'll cut to the chase and let you know where we stand. As you know, the DEA received a search warrant for your house in Spokane, Jenna."

"I know." She tensed, her face parchment pale, her freckles stark against her skin.

"I'm happy to report that nothing was found."

Jenna swayed, and Nikolai moved his hand from her shoulder to her waist, his fingers brushing against warm flesh as he steadied her. He should have pulled back, but didn't. Should have moved away, but couldn't.

"Don't you mean you're *sorry* that nothing was found? You've been painting Jenna as a criminal for days, and now your theories about her have to be thrown out the window. I think you owe her an apology." Nikolai didn't even try to hide his anger.

"An apology for what? We never accused Jenna of anything. We simply followed the leads where they took us. As a private investigator, I'm sure you understand that."

"From where I'm standing, it looks like there are several other directions you could have gone in."

"If you're talking about John Romero, then you should know that we've been conducting a thorough investigation. So far, there's nothing to indicate that he was involved in his wife's business with the Mexican Panthers."

"I really wish," Jenna said quietly, "that you'd stop talking about it as if that were a fact rather than a theory."

"Pardon me?" Officer Daniels looked genuinely surprised, and Nikolai almost felt sorry for him. To the officer, Jenna probably appeared fragile and near collapse, but there was fire in her eyes, and Nikolai had a feeling it wouldn't be long before Daniels realized just how ready for a fight she was.

"I said, that I wish you would stop talking as if Magdalena's involvement in drug trafficking is a fact. People in this country are innocent until proven guilty, and you've proven nothing."

"I'm afraid we don't see it the same way, Jenna. We have evidence that indicates—"

"I heard it all from Sergeant Anderson while he was holding us prisoner in his car for an hour and a half. I didn't believe it when he said it, and I don't believe it now."

"You weren't being held prisoner."

"Then what do you call it?"

"As I'm sure Anderson explained to you, we had evidence to collect before I was able to speak with you."

"You were trying to find evidence to arrest me, Officer Daniels. Just as you're trying to convince everyone who knew and loved Magdalena that she was a drug-addicted pawn of the Mexican Panthers. Just so you know, *I* won't believe it no matter how much evidence you collect."

"The problem with beliefs is that they aren't always based on facts."

"What facts? My friend traveled to Mexico three or four times a year to meet the needs of people who couldn't afford medical care for their children. There is not a person whose child she treated who would ever believe she'd dispense an unnecessary painkiller, let alone traffic in illegal narcotics." Though she didn't raise her voice, Jenna's anger spilled out into the sweet spring air, and Officer Daniels blinked as if seeing her for the first time.

"I understand how you feel, and if she were my friend, I'd feel the same way."

"But she wasn't your friend. You didn't watch her being dragged away by thugs. You didn't see the fear in her eyes, and you didn't hear her screaming for mercy. I couldn't save her, but I can preserve her memory. And I will. Now, if you'll excuse me, I really think I need to sit down." She took a step away, her body shaking so hard that Nikolai was afraid she'd fall over.

He scooped her into his arms, ignoring her protest as he carried her to his car and set her in the front seat.

"I could have walked," she mumbled, but her eyes were closed.

"Should I call an ambulance?" Officer Daniels hovered behind Nikolai, his concern obvious.

"I've got a migraine. An ambulance isn't going to help with that."

"How about a few hours of sleep, then?" Nikolai brushed silky hair from her forehead and looked into her eyes. They were glassy and vague, the blue faded and worn-looking.

"I want to talk to the DEA agents who are working Magdalena's case first."

"I wish I could say that was possible today, but their priority is to find the motorcyclist who tossed that hand grenade."

"Funny, the DEA was a lot more anxious to speak with me when they thought I was involved in drug trafficking." Jenna shifted, and Nikolai wondered if she planned to get out of the car and track down one of the agents.

"As I said, it's about priorities."

"If I weren't so sick, I'd go hunt someone down. As it is, you can let them know that I'll be at their office in the morning."

"You've got a flight out of town in the morning, Jen," Nikolai reminded her. And he had every intention of making sure she was on it.

"We'll see," she said, and he could hear the argument in her voice. He let it go. There'd be time enough to convince her when she was feeling better.

"I'll tell the agent in charge. I'm sure she'll be happy to speak with you as soon as she has time."

"I hope so. I want to find out why Magdalena was targeted by the Panthers, and then I want to get back to my life." She closed her eyes again, leaning her head against the seat.

Nikolai closed the door gently and took a few steps away from the car.

"Obviously, Jenna isn't up to answering questions," he said to Daniels.

"We have the statement she gave to Sergeant Anderson. That's enough for now."

"Jenna also isn't up to *asking* questions, so I'm going to ask a few for her." No way was he going to leave before he knew what the Houston PD's plan was for keeping Jenna safe.

"Shoot."

"Jenna has been attacked twice since Magdalena's funeral. How are you going to keep it from happening again?"

"We're doing everything we can to find the person responsible for the latest attack. We've been questioning the man who tried to shoot her. Unfortunately, he's not talking. That leaves us with almost nothing to go on."

"You've got plenty to go on. You know that Jenna was abducted by the Mexican Panthers. You know that has something to do with her friend Magdalena."

"What we don't know is why the Panthers are still coming after Jenna. Our sources are saying they've given up the chase. The DEA has undercover agents down in Mexico who are reporting the same thing. All the noise we're hearing indicates that she's in the clear."

"But she's not."

"No," Daniels took off his hat and ran a hand over his hair. "She's not. There's another facet to this that we're not seeing. Something we're missing. Until we find it, there's no way we can guarantee that she won't be attacked again."

"And you've checked Magdalena's husband thoroughly?"

"We've dug up some limited dirt, but nothing that points to criminal activity."

"What kind of dirt?"

"He has several girlfriends. Maybe even a child with another woman. We're still looking into it, but as far as anything else, he's clean."

"How about the people who were working at the clinic in Mexico?"

"We checked everyone, and we came up with nothing."

"Except proof that Magdalena was trafficking drugs?"

"That we *do* have. There were traces of cocaine found in storage crates used to ship supplies to and from the clinic. There were also traces of strong spices that traffickers use to blow the drug sniffing dogs' sense of smell. The more we search, the more it seems like this was a long-standing operation."

"Someone else could have been spearheading it," Nikolai said.

"Dr. Romero was responsible for ordering and packing all the supplies. She always took charge of unloading and loading the shipments."

"Jenna said John Romero helped with that."

"That's true, but Magdalena was head honcho, so to speak. She told him what to do, and he did it."

"According to John?"

"According to other people who were involved in financing the clinic."

"So you did the math and found Magdalena guilty and her husband innocent."

"As I said to Jenna, we build our cases on facts. We have the facts, and if Magdalena were alive, it would be enough to put her away for years."

"Jenna is convinced the facts are erroneous. She believes her friend is innocent."

"She's loyal. It's a good quality, but it doesn't always pay off." Daniels glanced at his watch and scowled. "I've got a meeting with the team in ten. We're going to have a patrol car stationed outside of the Romeros', but let Jenna know that she should take extra precautions."

"I will."

"I'll call you if we get any new leads."

"Thanks." Nikolai watched the officer walk away, feeling

more frustrated than he had been when they'd begun the conversation.

Daniels was right. There was something missing. Some piece of the puzzle that needed to be found and put into place. Only then would they see the full picture and understand exactly where Jenna fit into it all.

He walked around to the driver's side of the car and slid in behind the wheel. He wanted to start driving and keep driving, taking Jenna as far away from Houston as he could get her. But he'd learned a long time ago that running from problems didn't solve them. He'd learned to face things head-on rather than turning his back on them.

And that's exactly what he planned to do now.

Magdalena was the key to the attacks against Jenna. There was no doubt about that. What Nikolai needed to find out was why Magdalena had been killed. Not drugs. If that had been the case, Jenna would be safe and the point would be moot, the Panthers content to let an innocent woman escape. There was something else, and Nikolai couldn't shake the feeling that Magdalena's husband was the key.

"You look grim," Jenna said, her voice barely carrying over the sound of the car engine. He glanced at her, saw that she was watching him through heavy-lidded eyes.

"Were you sleeping?"

"You're avoiding the question."

"I didn't realize you'd asked one."

"Okay. I'll rephrase. Why do you look so grim?"

"Today shouldn't have happened."

"Every day happens, Nikolai."

"Yeah, but every day doesn't have a hand grenade–tossing motorcyclist in it."

"Or a gunman."

"That's exactly my point. If the Panthers were really after you, you'd have died in Mexico."

"That's a cheerful thought."

"You survived. You made it over the border. You spent five

days in a hospital, two days in a hotel and nothing happened. No gunmen lurking in shadows. No bombs. No knife attacks. There are a thousand ways you could have been killed and probably several dozen opportunities to do it, but you were left alone."

"Until the day of Magdalena's funeral."

"Right. She's buried and then you're attacked three times in two days. Why?"

"If I knew that, this would all be over and I'd be sitting at home, Dante warming my feet."

"You'll be there soon, Jen." He patted her knee, let his hand settle there.

She didn't move away, didn't even try to pretend that she didn't want the connection as much as he did.

For a moment, silence enveloped them both. Then Jenna placed her hand over his so that their fingers twined. "In case I don't get another chance to say it, Nikolai, I think I'm doing exactly what I didn't want to do."

"What's that?"

"Falling for you." She squeezed his hand, released it.

"Should I be upset about that?"

"No, but I probably should be."

"Why?"

"Because when this is over, I'll go back to my life and you'll go back to yours, and my life will feel a whole lot emptier than it did when you were in it," she said.

"Who says I won't be in it?"

"Isn't that the way these things always go? People meet under the most extraordinary of circumstances. They fall for each other. They have a brief and volatile relationship, and then it's over."

"Brief and volatile, huh?"

"Oh, come on, I'm sure you've watched enough movies to know it's true."

"I'm not much of a movie buff. I prefer to live my life rather than to watch fictional lives play out on-screen." He pulled up in front of the Romero house, letting the car idle as he turned to face Jenna.

She'd closed her eyes again, and if Nikolai hadn't known better, he would have thought she was asleep.

"Jen?"

"Yeah?" She looked into his eyes, her gaze hazy with pain and fatigue.

"I'm not comfortable leaving you here. I don't like John, and I don't trust him."

"And?"

"How about we pack your things and move you to my place?"

"I don't think that's a good idea."

"Why not?"

"I already told you. You and me alone in your apartment just doesn't seem right."

"We're not kids, Jen. I think we can handle it for a night."

"I'm sure we can, but I'm not sure we should."

"You've spent the night in John's house."

"John isn't you." She blushed, her cheeks going bright pink.

"Okay. So, I'll stay here. If he's really an upstanding citizen and good friend, I'm sure John will be willing to put your bodyguard up for the night."

"Bodyguard? You're kidding, right?"

"Do I look like I am?"

"I can't tell. Only one of my eyes is working well."

"You're losing your vision again? I'd better call the doctor." He pulled out his cell phone, but Jenna put a hand on his arm.

"I'm fine. It's just part of the whole migraine thing."

"You're sure?" He put a hand on her forehead, felt cool, dry skin.

"Yes. I'll just take some medicine and lie down for a while." She seemed to have forgotten his comment about being her bodyguard, and he didn't bother bringing it up again. He knew what needed to be done to keep her safe, and he had every intention of doing it.

He walked her around to the side of the house, taking keys from her fumbling fingers and opening the door to the guest suite. The lights were off, and he kept them that way, leading her into the bedroom and watching as she threw herself facedown onto the bed.

"Where's your medicine?"

"On the table near the sofa." She didn't bother lifting her head as she spoke, and the words were mumbled through fabric and pillow.

He found the bottle where she'd left it, tipped a pill into his hand and grabbed a glass of water. By the time he returned to the room, Jenna had kicked off her shoes and was sitting on the edge of the bed.

"Here you go."

"Thanks." She took the pill, gulping down the water and setting the glass on a bedside table. Then she eased back down onto the bed and turned her face back into the pillow.

Nikolai should have left then, but something held him in place. Maybe it was the sight of silky red hair lying against the white pillowcase. Maybe it was the fragility of Jenna's shoulders and back, the too-thin curve of her hip and thigh. She looked vulnerable, like someone who could easily be broken. Not just physically, but emotionally.

She must have sensed his gaze. She turned her head, eyeing him with a scowl that would have sent tougher men running.

"Just so you know, Nikolai. I may be crazy enough to fall for you, but I'm not crazy enough to let you see me at my worst. Go do something, because I can't moan and groan and cry with you hovering beside the bed."

"Is that what you're planning to do?" he asked, running his knuckles down her cheek, and smiling again when she shivered in response.

"I haven't decided yet. Now, go away so I can think about it." She turned her face to the pillow again, dismissing him with a finality he couldn't ignore.

He grabbed a throw from the end of the bed, placed it over Jenna and left the room.

Left the room, but he wouldn't go far.

There was no way he'd leave Jenna alone there. There'd already been three attempts on her life. Four if he counted the one in Mexico. He intended to make sure he was around if whoever was trying to kill her tried again.

He pulled out his cell phone, walking to the door and stepping outside. He didn't have a laptop and couldn't do much by way of research, but he could make some phone calls. Maybe Skylar had discovered something that would help clear up the case. One way or another, Nikolai would keep digging, keep searching. Eventually, he'd find the truth. He could only pray that he could keep Jenna safe until he did.

EIGHTEEN

Jenna woke with a start, her heart racing, the sound of a ringing phone sinking into her consciousness.

She stumbled from the bedroom, grabbing the receiver and pressing it to her ear. "Hello?"

"Jenna? It's John. I thought I'd call and check in since you didn't make it to the park this morning. Is everything okay?"

"There was a problem when Nikolai and I went to breakfast." She filled him in quickly, searching the living room for Nikolai. He was gone. Which shouldn't have disappointed her, but did.

"Wow! That's crazy. Did they find the guy?"

"Not yet." At least she didn't think they had. She pulled out her cell phone, scrolling through the incoming calls, hoping to find one from the police. There wasn't one.

"Well, I'm glad you're okay. I was worried. You and Magdalena were such good friends, and I know she'd want me to treat you like the sister she always felt you were."

"I appreciate that, John. Is Ben still asking for her?"

"Yes. I think he will be for a while. They were really close, the two of them. He was Magdalena's shadow."

"I remember. Everywhere she went, he was right on her heels." The memories made Jenna smile, and she walked across the room, closing curtains to prevent light from spilling into the room. Despite the medicine she'd taken, her head was still throbbing, and the sunlight was like a hot poker stabbing into her eyes.

"Yeah. I was second best when she was around, but I didn't mind. She was a great mother and deserved all the affection."

A soft tap sounded on the exterior door, and Jenna swung toward it, a scream catching in her throat as it opened.

"Jen? Is everything okay?" John asked as Nikolai stepped into the room.

"Fine. Nikolai just walked in, and I was distracted."

"I see."

"See what?"

"You two are moving pretty fast, aren't you?"

"I'm not sure that's any of your business." Surprised, Jenna met Nikolai's gaze, wondering if he'd heard John's comment.

He mouthed John's name, and she nodded.

"I suppose it's not. As I said, though, Magdalena would have wanted me to look out for you, and, to be honest, I'm not that fond of your new friend."

"I don't think he's very fond of you, either."

"I got that impression. Though I'm not sure what I did to offend him." The comment begged a response, but Jenna refused to give one.

"I'm really sorry that I missed spending time at the park with your family, John. I hope Ben wasn't too disappointed."

"He's three. His disappointments don't last long."

"Still, I would have loved to spend time with him. We've got so little time left before I return home."

"That reminds me. I had another reason for calling. Magdalena's lawyer called while I was at the park. He needs to postpone the reading of the will until tomorrow afternoon. There's been an emergency in the family, and he has to be out of town for the night."

"I hope everyone is all right."

"His son broke a collarbone during a hockey match but should recover fully."

"I'm glad to hear it, but sorry the reading has been postponed. My plane leaves in the morning, and I plan to be on it."

"I can have the ticket switched for you. I'm sure the airline will understand the extenuating circumstances."

"They might, but it's not something I'm willing to do." She'd had enough of Houston. Enough of intrigue and danger. She wanted to go home to her safe and predictable life, and she could only pray that when she did danger wouldn't follow her there.

"It would have meant so much to Magdalena," he said. It was the same argument he'd used the previous day, but this time it didn't sway Jenna. She'd loved her friend, but she couldn't continue to put herself in danger for someone who was already safe in the arms of the Lord.

"I know, and I wish I could be here for it, but I can't."

"Give it some more thought. You have nearly fifteen hours before your plane leaves. Maybe you'll change your mind."

Before she could respond, Nikolai pulled the phone from her hand and pressed it to his ear. "John, it's Nikolai. I'm sure Jenna told you about the morning she's had."

He paused, his dark eyes staring into Jenna's as he listened to John's reply.

"Yes. I understand your point, but Jenna is ready to go home. She's made that abundantly clear, and I think you'd be wise not to pressure her about it." He crooked his finger, urging Jenna to move closer to the phone.

She did, stepping into his arms and leaning her head toward the phone so she could clearly hear John's words.

"I can't say I blame her. The past week has been pretty harrowing. Are you two still planning to come for dinner, or is she too worn out?"

Nikolai raised an eyebrow, and Jenna nodded.

"We'll be there."

"Great. I'll see you around five. Sorry it's going to be early, but Ben goes to bed at seven."

"No problem. We'll see you then." Nikolai disconnected, holding the phone in his hand for a long moment before he placed it back in the cradle.

"Pretty fancy, this," he said.

"What?"

"You're in the same house, but he uses a phone to communicate."

"It's a good way to give his guests privacy."

"True. Feeling better?" he asked as he wrapped an arm around her waist and tugged her against his side. Being there felt so good, so natural that Jenna didn't even pretend she wanted to move away.

She'd told him that she thought she was falling for him, but that had been a lie. She'd already fallen, and she wasn't sure she'd ever be able to get back up.

"A little. Was I out for long?"

"A couple of hours."

"It felt like minutes."

"You needed the rest." His hand smoothed up her back and down again, and it was all she could do not to snuggle close, let herself imagine that what they had could last.

"Did you go back to your place?"

"I was outside. I had a few phone calls to make."

"Should I ask to whom?"

"A colleague of mine was doing some research for me. I asked her to question some of Magdalena's college and high school friends."

"And?"

"There wasn't a person among the group who had anything negative to say. Magdalena was well-liked and admired by her peers."

"I could have told you that was what they'd say."

"There were a few things that came up, though."

"What?" She moved away, wanting to face him full-on when he told her what could only be bad news.

"Two of her high school friends had contact with her several times a month and felt they knew her well. Both said they'd been concerned about her in the months preceding the trip to Mexico. According to them, she hadn't seemed like herself. I was wondering if you had the same feeling."

Had she?

With everything that had happened in the past week, Jenna hadn't spent much time thinking about the weeks and months preceding the mission trip. But there *had* been some things that had seemed off. A few instances when Magdalena hadn't returned calls or e-mails. A couple of conversations in which she'd mentioned being overwhelmed and tired. That hadn't been typical of Magdalena, but it also hadn't seemed overly alarming.

"She did seem more tense than usual. I chalked it up to the scope of the trip. She was doubling the number of medical professionals who were working at the clinic, and she increased the time in the country by a week."

"Did she say why?"

"The need was always greater than her capacity to meet it, but she felt she had to try." Those had been her exact words, and Jenna could still hear Magdalena's voice saying them.

"What about when she was in Mexico?"

"She was tired, but excited to be there."

"So, she didn't seem tense or unhappy while she was there?"

"No, but there were a couple of times when she seemed… sad. I asked her if something was wrong, but she insisted that she was just tired. Maybe I should have pushed for more of an answer."

"If she did have something on her mind, you couldn't have known how serious it might be."

"You're right, but that doesn't make me feel any better."

She sighed, walking into the kitchen and rinsing out the coffee pot. "Want some coffee?"

"Actually, I was thinking more along the lines of lunch."

"We just ate."

"Hours ago. I need to refuel."

"There's food in the fridge. Want me to make you something?"

"You make your coffee. I'll see what there is to eat." He walked into the kitchen, taking up much more than his fair share of space. Jenna couldn't move without bumping into him, and by the time she had coffee brewing, her cheeks were flaming.

"You look flushed. You're not sick, are you?" Nikolai pressed a cool palm to her cheek, and that was it. Just one touch and Jenna was lost, her heart racing, her skin tingling. She tried to step back, her hip banging into the counter, her lungs expanding to take in more of Nikolai's masculine scent.

She wanted to lean closer, wanted to run away.

She put her hand up, pressing it against his chest. She meant to hold him at a distance, meant to tell him that they needed to slow down and think things through, but his skin was warm through his T-shirt, his heart beating strong and steady beneath her palm.

"Jen?" It was a question and a request. It was Nikolai, being Nikolai, giving her every opportunity to pull them both out of the fire they were about to fall into.

But she didn't.

His hand moved from her cheek to her neck, his fingers skimming along the tender flesh beneath her jaw. And then he was bending down, his lips brushing hers, tasting her fear and her longing.

She gasped, her fingers weaving through his hair, her body humming with the sheer pleasure of Nikolai's touch. She let her hand trail down his neck to his shoulders, felt the corded muscles beneath his shirt and wanted more.

She broke away, gasping for breath, her hand trembling as she raised her fingers to her lips.

What had they done?

What had *she* done?

Falling for Nikolai was one thing, falling into his arms was quite another. "We shouldn't—"

"We did, so let's not ruin it with regrets."

"But—"

"You're going to ruin it, aren't you?" He smiled gently, and Jenna's gaze dropped to his lips, rested there for a moment too long.

"No." She looked away, focusing on the counter, the cabinets, the stove, anything but Nikolai's face.

"But you do have regrets."

"I just don't want to fall too far, Nikolai. I don't want to start believing in happily-ever-afters and forevers. And I know I will. That's just the kind of person I am."

"You make it sound like that's a bad thing."

"It can be."

"Not if the person you're falling for is falling with you. Not if the man you want those things with wants them, too." He tucked her hair behind her ear, his fingers tracing the curve of her ear, then following the line of her jaw to her chin and up to her lips.

"We barely know each other," she added.

"We survived nearly certain death together. I think we know each other as well as we know anyone else."

"Nikolai—" A loud knock sounded from down the hall, and Jenna jumped, whirling to face the sound.

"It's the door into the main house. I'll get it." Nikolai walked through the small hallway and pulled the door open, stepping aside as John's mother walked in carrying a large tray.

"I'm so sorry for barging in on you, but I made some chicken noodle soup for lunch today, and John thought you might like some. He said you were under the weather." Mrs.

Romero spoke in a rush of words, her tight salt-and-pepper curls vibrating. Short and a little plump, she looked nothing like John or his debonair father.

"That's very kind of you, Mrs. Romero."

"It was no problem at all. I always make too much when I cook, so there's plenty. Come sit at the table. Both of you. It's best eaten when it's hot." She set the tray on the table and lifted a cobalt soup bowl from it. "Now, Jenna, this one is for you. John insisted on dishing it up in one of Magdalena's favorite bowls. Handmade in Mexico by the mother of one of her patients. John said she'd want you to have it, so once you finish eating, we'll just wash it out and pack it for you to take home."

"I couldn't—"

"My dear, Magdalena is no longer here to enjoy that bowl. She would much rather you have it than for it to sit in a cupboard, never used."

It was true. That was the kind of woman Magdalena had been. She loved things to be useful and used, and she hated for anything to be wasted.

"Thank you, then."

"Don't thank me. As I said, it was John's idea. Though how he can think past his grief, I don't know." She shook her head and wiped at her eyes.

"It must be incredibly hard on all of you." Jenna took a seat at the table, not meeting Nikolai's eyes as he sat across from her.

They'd kissed, and she could still taste him on her lips.

Just the thought made her blush again, and she grabbed a dinner roll from a basket Mrs. Romero held out and smeared butter on it.

Anything to keep from looking at Nikolai.

"It is. I never had a daughter, and Magdalena was one to me. Such a sweet and loving girl. So giving." She dropped down into a chair, apparently content to sit and watch while Jenna and Nikolai ate.

"Your son doesn't seem quite as convinced of her sweetness," Nikolai said, and Jenna kicked his shin, hoping to get him to keep quiet. He grinned, but kept right on talking. "He seems to think she was involved in drug trafficking."

"He's said as much to me, too, but I think it's the grief talking. There's no way Magdalena was involved in any of those things, and I told John as much."

"Did you tell the police that?" Jenna asked, and Mrs. Romero nodded.

"Of course. I couldn't have Magdalena's name besmirched. Eat your soup, dear. It's going to get cold."

Jenna spooned up a mouthful of soup, surprised at the flavorful broth. "It's delicious."

"Thank you. It was John's special request. He's always loved my chicken noodle soup. It's a comfort food for him, I think."

"I can see why. If I'd grown up eating this, I'd be requesting it during times of trouble, too." Jenna ate another spoonful, her stomach lurching in protest. Between the migraine and the medicine Jenna had taken, there wasn't much hope that she'd finish the bowl of soup. She gave it a try, though, scooping more into her mouth and hoping she looked like she was enjoying it.

"For John, things like this soup are incredibly important. He does tend to hold things in. But, as I've always told him, bottling things up is no way to deal with them."

"You think he's bottling up his feelings about Magdalena?" Nikolai asked, apparently determined to continue his impromptu interview.

"Of course. He's devastated. He loved her, after all, but he won't cry in front of his son. Says it will upset Benjamin too much."

"So, there were no problems between Magdalena and John?"

"You sound like the police, young man. And I'll tell you the same thing I told them—no marriage is perfect. Magdalena and John had their fair share of problems, but they always worked them out."

"So, they were both committed to making the marriage work?"

"Absolutely. As a matter of fact, John was so committed to it that he suggested accompanying Magdalena on her mission trip to Mexico."

"Really?" Surprised, Jenna put her spoon down and pushed the nearly empty bowl away. "Magdalena didn't mention that."

"Well, he did. He was involved in ordering supplies with her and packing things up. They really made quite a team."

"But he didn't end up going with her."

"True. At the last minute, they decided that they didn't want to leave little Benjamin without either parent for two weeks, so John stayed home."

"As I said, I'm surprised that Magdalena didn't mention it. She always said that she wished John would be more involved in her work in Mexico."

"It probably slipped her mind. Those trips took a lot out of her. Are you done with your soup?"

"Yes. I'm afraid I wasn't that hungry."

"You ate plenty. I'll go ahead and wash this out. Do you have a carry-on for the plane? I don't think keeping the bowl in your suitcase would be a good idea. I'd hate for it to break." Mrs. Romero bustled into the kitchen and set to work washing out the bowl.

"I can do that," Jenna hurried to her side but was motioned away.

"Go sit down, my dear. I know you're recovering from a terrible head injury. I'm sure you need plenty of rest."

"Washing a dish won't hurt me."

"It won't hurt me, either. Now, sit down at the table with your young man while I do this."

Her young man?

Was that what Nikolai was?

Was it what he wanted to be? What she wanted him to be?

Jenna's stomach twisted in knots at the questions, her throat tight and dry with anxiety. There was already too much to think about. She didn't need to add Nikolai to the mix.

Too late. You already have.

The words whispered through her mind as she took a seat across from Nikolai again. He met her gaze, offering a smile that lit up his face and warmed his eyes.

"This is great soup. Probably the best chicken noodle soup I've ever had," he said to John's mother, but his gaze never left Jenna's face.

"Oh my, you are a charmer. No wonder Jenna is so smitten with you."

"I'm not—"

"You're not going to ruin this moment, too, are you, Jenna?" Nikolai grinned, and she couldn't stop her answering smile.

"I guess I'll let it slide."

"Too bad. I was thinking if you decided to argue with Mrs. Romero, I might have to find a way to prove you wrong." His gaze dropped to her lips, and Jenna blushed.

"Sorry to disappoint you, but—" She paused as a wave of nausea hit, stealing her breath and her thoughts.

"Jenna?" Nikolai was up and around the table before Jenna realized he was moving, his face bent close to hers.

"Just the medicine and the migraine upsetting my stomach. I'll be fine." But it felt like a giant hand had reached in and twisted her gut, and she gasped, leaning forward to try to ease the pain.

"Take a deep breath. Try to relax."

"It's a little hard to relax when it feels like my insides are being torn apart." She gasped again, the pain intensifying so that it was the only thing she knew.

"She doesn't look good at all." Mrs. Romero's voice seeped through the pain, and Jenna tried to tell her she was fine, but the words wouldn't form.

Cool hands pressed against her forehead and her cheeks, a wet rag cooled the back of her neck, but the pain didn't recede. Instead, it grew in red waves of agony until Jenna wasn't sure where one pain ended and another began.

She reached out, grabbing Nikolai's hand, her heart skipping a beat, the rhythm erratic and unnatural.

"Something's wrong," she managed to say, her throat tightening on the words, fear suddenly as real as the pain.

"It's okay. You're going to be fine." But she could see the panic in his eyes, see the worry etching deep lines on either side of his mouth.

"Of course, I am." She forced the words out, forced herself to stand, to take a step away just to prove the point.

Another pain hit, slamming into her abdomen, stealing her thoughts and her strength. She could feel nothing else. Not her legs. Not her feet.

"Jen—" Nikolai's voice was the last thing she heard as she fell into darkness.

NINETEEN

Nikolai paced the small waiting room, his muscles tense with worry. It had been nearly three hours since the ambulance had brought Jenna to the hospital, and the doctor still hadn't come out to tell Nikolai how she was doing.

He was ready to walk through the double doors and search the triage area until he found her.

"Nikolai?" John Romero walked into the room, his eyes dark with worry. "How is she?"

"I don't know."

"I wish I could have gotten here sooner. Ben was having a rough time, and my mom didn't feel comfortable staying with him."

"No problem." As a matter of fact, Nikolai would have preferred that John stay away altogether. The guy had been less than useless when Jenna was nearly convulsed with pain in his guest suite. He'd stood a few feet away, offering little more than a few grimaces of distaste while his mother and Nikolai had done what they could to make her comfortable.

But there'd been nothing they could do, and that had eaten at Nikolai for the past few hours. He'd seen Jenna when she was trussed up and blind in Mexico. He'd watched her struggle against pain and fear and grief, but he'd never seen her as she'd been in the moments before the ambulance arrived—completely helpless and unable to fight.

He never wanted to see her like that again.

"What do you think is going on? I mean, she looked bad. I don't think I've ever seen someone in so much pain." John's words cut into his thoughts, and Nikolai met the other man's eyes.

"I don't know. I'm hoping the doctors can figure it out." Nikolai kept his voice neutral as he took a few steps away from John. He didn't want to have a long drawn-out conversation with the guy. What he wanted was to find Jenna and make sure she was okay.

"Maybe it has something to do with the head injury she suffered. Those things are notorious for causing unexpected complications."

"Look, John," he swung toward the guy, saw the other man had the glassy-eyed look of someone in shock and gentled his tone. "I don't know what's wrong with Jenna. I'm hoping a doctor is going to walk in here and tell us at any moment, but until one does, I'd prefer not to speculate."

John nodded, dropping into a chair a few feet away. "Sorry. I know it doesn't help. It's what I did when I learned that Magdalena was missing. I came up with a million places she could be. None of them were where she was finally found."

"You must miss your wife terribly." Nikolai threw out the bait by rote, not really caring to hear John's response. Someone needed to walk through the double doors and tell him what was going on with Jenna, and that someone needed to do it now.

"The truth is that I don't." John's words were so unexpected that Nikolai thought he'd heard them wrong.

"Pardon me?"

"I said that I don't miss her." John stood and shrugged, his gaze jumping from Nikolai to a bank of windows across the room.

"That's a big change from what you told me before."

"No, it isn't. I loved my wife, but she was difficult. She demanded all my time and attention, and, to be brutally honest, every bit of my patience. I'm sad she's gone, but I don't miss her. The house is lighter without her in it."

"And you're telling me this now because...?"

"I asked for a divorce shortly before she left for Mexico. I hadn't filed any papers, but I figure with all the digging you're doing, you may hear about it from one of Magdalena's friends. I don't want you to get the wrong idea."

"What would that be?"

"That I hated her. That I wanted her dead. I didn't. All I wanted was a little peace."

"Now you have it."

"Yeah, but I wish I could have gotten it another way." He rubbed the back of his neck, and Nikolai almost believed he was telling the truth.

Almost.

"Did you mention this to the police?"

"What do you think? My wife was brutally murdered. The husband is always the first suspect."

"And usually the best one."

"I did *not* kill my wife."

"Let's say you didn't. Let's say you simply wanted a divorce. I still don't understand why you're bringing this up now. You've had days to come clean, and you chose this moment. I want to know why."

"A friend called me an hour ago. Someone has been calling around, asking about the state of my marriage. I figured that had something to do with you. I wanted to give you the facts, so you wouldn't have to keep bothering my friends." He said it with venom, the anger in his eyes hot and ugly, the change in his demeanor as surprising as his confession had been.

"I see."

"No. You don't. I'm ready to move on with my life. The police are willing to let me. My family is willing to let me. I'd really appreciate it if you would let me, too."

"Sorry, I can't do that. Jenna asked me to prove Magdalena's innocence. That's what I'm going to do."

"Mr. Jansen?" A petite blond stepped into the room, her lab coat and stethoscope giving her away as a doctor. "I'm Dr. Santino. I've been caring for Jenna Dougherty."

"How is she?" He rushed toward her, not caring about John's confession or his venom or his reasons for either.

"Stable. It was touch and go for a while."

"Touch and go?" John stepped up beside Nikolai, offering a handshake and introduction.

"She had some uneven heart rhythms. We were afraid that she'd go into cardiac arrest."

"What caused it?" John asked the next question before Nikolai could think past the image of Jenna lying in a hospital bed, her heart refusing to beat normally, the doctors struggling to stabilize her.

"We don't know. It could be a reaction to the medicine she took for her migraine. Some people's systems can't handle certain chemicals. How long was it between the time she took it and the time she began having symptoms?"

"A few hours."

"That's what she said, too." The doctor frowned.

"Does that make a reaction less likely?"

"Less likely, but not impossible. We're running some blood tests and we've done a CAT scan of her abdomen. Everything looks good so far."

"Can I see her?" Nikolai hoped the doctor said yes, because he planned to see Jenna whether he got permission or not.

"She's been asking for you for an hour. We just got her settled into a room. I'll walk you up. I'm afraid she can only have one visitor at a time."

"I'll get a cup of coffee then." John hurried away, and Nikolai followed the doctor through the double doors and into the triage area. It was ripe with the scent of antiseptic and illness. Somewhere, a baby was crying and a man and a woman were arguing. Typical E.R. scene, and one Nikolai would be happy to put behind him.

"This way. Next time you come up, you can take the elevator

in the main lobby. She's on the second floor." The doctor led him into a service elevator and pushed the button.

"How long will she be here?"

"If the all the tests come back normal and she remains stable tonight, we'll release her in the morning."

"She has a flight out of Houston tomorrow."

"So she keeps telling me. I guess she's anxious to go home. Hopefully, we'll be able to allow that." The doctor smiled as the elevator doors opened.

"Did Jenna explain that she's been attacked several times in the past few days?"

"She did. We're doing a few tests to find out if she's been exposed to poison of any kind. Those will take a day or two to come back."

"Are her symptoms consistent with that?"

"Consistent enough that I've called the police, but not conclusive. As I said, she could have had a severe reaction to the medicine she took."

"She's taken the medicine before."

"Generally speaking, people have a worse reaction the second time they're exposed to something. Here we are." She knocked on a door and opened it.

Nikolai followed her into the small room, his eyes riveted to the empty bed. "She's gone."

"I'm not gone. Though I'd really like to be on a plane heading home rather than stuck in this hospital room." Jenna stepped out of the bathroom, her face dewy with moisture.

She looked shaky and pale but better than she had a few hours before.

"You should be in bed, Jenna." The doctor frowned, and Nikolai took Jenna's arm, offering her support as she dropped into a chair.

"I wanted to splash some cold water on my face. I was starting to drift off."

"You should have let yourself." Nikolai poured a cup of

ice water from a carafe, offering it to her, but Jenna shook her head.

"I can't. I'm afraid if I put anything in my stomach, I'll be back where I was a few hours ago." She held out her hand, and he took it, squeezing gently, alarmed by the cold, clammy feel of her skin.

"You're still in pain?"

"Some."

"That should subside soon," the doctor said. "Now, how about you get back in bed, and we hook you up to the heart monitor? I'd like to see how you're doing now that you've been up and around."

"No palpitations, if that's what you're asking. My heart seems to be doing just fine."

"Humor me, anyway." Dr. Santino gestured to the bed, and Jenna stood reluctantly.

"I feel like an old woman. Every muscle in my body hurts."

"Hopefully, that will ease in a few hours, too. If you'll step outside, Mr. Jansen, I'll get Jenna hooked up and check her heart. Then you can visit for a while."

Nikolai didn't want to leave the room and was tempted to simply turn his back, but Jenna shot him an impatient look, and he respected her too much to stay when she obviously wanted him to leave. "I'll be right outside."

He stepped into the hall, nearly barreling into Officer Daniels.

"Sorry about that. I've been kicked out of the room for a few minutes." He pulled the door shut and turned to face the officer.

"How is she?"

"Alive. Which is a lot more than I thought she'd be. It's been a long time since I've seen anyone so sick." And a longer time since he'd felt so completely out of control, so absolutely dependent on God's mercy.

"We got a call from a doctor here. She said poison is suspected."

"Either that or Jenna had a bad reaction to her migraine medicine."

"What's your gut feeling on it?"

"Jenna had homemade chicken noodle soup right before she collapsed. I'd like to know what was in it."

"I'll send someone to the Romeros' house and have the dish it was served in taken as evidence."

"I don't know if that will help. John's mother washed the dish after Jenna ate."

"Doesn't matter. There are usually traces of poison left if it's been used, so we'll check that out, and we'll question the family."

"John is here. He showed up a half hour ago."

"I'll find him after I speak to you and Jenna. Want to tell me what happened?"

Nikolai nodded, quickly filling the officer in.

When he was finished, Daniels leaned a shoulder against the wall and frowned. "The more I hear about this case, the less sense it makes."

"I agree. The only constant in any of it is that someone wants Jenna dead."

"If Jenna *was* poisoned, that someone had access to the Romero house and to the food she was served. Which really limits the number of suspects. I'm going to call this in. Maybe Romero will give us permission to search his house. If he doesn't, I'll get a warrant." He pulled the radio from his belt and called in the report.

When he finished, Nikolai met his eyes and smiled grimly. "It looks like we're finally heading in the same direction, Daniels."

"If we are, it's because I'm following the leads just as I've always done. Eventually, doing so always takes me in the right direction."

"Let's hope it takes you there quickly. I'm not sure Jenna can survive another attack."

"God willing, she won't have to."

Nikolai hoped and prayed He was. *Believed* He was.

There was no other option.

"Did you get any information on the hand grenade or the guy who tossed it?"

"The hand grenade was World War II vintage. Easy to get if you know where to look. Shouldn't have been live, which is why it didn't explode when it hit the ground. There were explosives in it, though. I'd call it a modified pipe bomb."

"Whatever it was, it could have done some serious damage if it *had* exploded."

"True, and when we find the guy who tossed it, he'll be booked on terrorism charges. Whether or not we can make them stick remains to be seen."

"Is there any way to trace the grenade?"

"We've got a partial serial number, but tracing it is going to take time."

"We're all set in here." The doctor opened the door and stepped into the hallway. "Heart rate is good. It looks like Jenna may be able to leave in the morning."

"I *will* be leaving in the morning." Jenna called out, and Nikolai had no doubt that she and the doctor had differing opinions about the matter.

The doctor ignored her comment, just offered a quick wave and a promise to be by early in the morning.

"I can't believe she actually thinks I might stay here an extra day." Jenna sat on the edge of the bed, her jeaned legs hanging out from under a blue-green hospital gown. Her feet were bare, bright red polish on her toenails.

"If it will ensure your health, then it's for the best." Nikolai walked into the room, Officer Daniels right behind him.

"I'm not sure ensuring my health is possible at this point, and, the way I see it, if I'm going to face death, I'd rather do it at home." She stood, crossing to the window and staring out into the darkening evening.

"Jenna, are you up to answering a few questions? If we keep digging, we might figure out what's going on, put the person responsible in jail and really ensure your safety." Officer Daniels pulled out a small notebook as Jenna nodded.

"I've answered dozens of questions in the past week, and you still haven't found the person responsible."

"We will. As I said to Nikolai, it's just a matter of time."

"Time is something I'm beginning to think I don't have a lot of." Jenna dropped onto the bed again, anxiety and frustration pulsing out from her in waves.

Nikolai crossed to her side, taking a seat beside her, and putting an arm around her shoulders. She smiled, but the fear was still in her eyes.

"It's going to be okay, Jenna."

"You're always telling me that."

"Because I'm always believing it. God hasn't saved you over and over again to let you die now."

"I hope not."

"I *know* not." He squeezed her hand gently, praying he was right. As much as he believed that God was in control, Nikolai had never claimed to understand His ways. Why one person lived a long life and another died young, why one person was born into poverty and another into riches were things that Nikolai would never comprehend. What he did understand was that there was power in prayer and that faith was all that was needed to see a person through the most trying of circumstances.

He prayed as Officer Daniels questioned Jenna, prayed more as the officer left to find Romero and continued to pray as Jenna sprawled back on the bed and closed her eyes.

When his cell phone rang, he ignored it, determined to stay by Jenna's side as she slept. When it rang again, he glanced at the caller ID and frowned. John Romero.

Nikolai covered Jenna with an extra blanket and walked

out into the hall. It was quiet, the hospital settling down for the night.

"Hello?"

"What kind of game are you playing, Jansen?"

"Maybe if you explain what you're talking about, I can tell you." He leaned a shoulder against the wall, more pleased than he probably should be to hear John's frantic tone. It was past time for the guy to get flustered and start worrying.

"The police are at my house, going through my cupboards. Apparently, you thought it would be funny to tell them that I'd poisoned Jenna."

"That isn't what I told them."

"Then why are they here?"

"Jenna was fine. Then she ate soup that your mother prepared and you dished up, and she wasn't fine. Do the math." Feet tapped on the tile floor and a custodian moved past, mop and bucket in hand.

Nikolai took a step closer to Jenna's door.

"So, you're saying my *mother* tried to murder Jenna?"

"I'm not saying anything." The tap of the custodian's feet on the tile had ceased, the hall eerie in its silence. Nikolai tensed, barely listening as John continued to complain. Something was wrong. He felt it and turned as the custodian lunged toward him, what looked like a police club in his hand. Nikolai put up an arm to fend off the first blow, felt the bone snap as the club hit.

There was no time to feel pain.

No time to do anything but fight.

He dodged as the club swung toward his head, grabbing for his attacker's arm, twisting it, Nikolai's one good arm no match for the other man's strength.

The club swung again, the heavy wood crashing into Nikolai's temple. He felt a moment of rage, a moment of pure fear for Jenna and then he felt nothing at all.

TWENTY

Shuffling. Sliding. Fabric dragging on the floor.

The sounds drifted into Jenna's dreams, and for a moment she was back in Mexico, lying on the cement floor of the old house, waiting to learn her fate. She jerked upright, her heart pounding as she caught sight of a dark figure near the room's door.

"Nikolai?" It was too dark to see much detail, but she could make out dark hair and a slim build. Not Nikolai, then. A doctor, maybe. Or a nurse.

"He went for some coffee. I told him I'd keep an eye on you until he returned."

"That's not necessary." She felt uneasy, but wasn't sure why. Nikolai had every right to go for a cup of coffee, and she had no reason to doubt the word of the man walking toward her.

No reason except for the fact that someone wants you dead.

The thought whispered through her mind as the man took a few steps closer, his eyes gleaming in the darkness. "Probably not, but I doubt your boyfriend would thank me if I left you here alone."

"It's not his decision to make, and I really would prefer to be alone." She tried to put some strength in her voice, but the words came out weak and tentative.

"You're due for your medicine anyway, so it isn't a bother

for me to spend a few minutes with you." He pulled a syringe from his pocket, and Jenna's eyes widened.

"What medicine?"

"Pain meds."

"The doctor didn't say anything about that."

"It probably just slipped his mind."

"Her. My doctor is a woman."

"That's right. Sorry, I just came on shift an hour ago." He smiled, flashing white teeth and cold, hard eyes as he uncapped the syringe, opened the port on the IV.

"I think I'll skip it." Jenna yanked the IV stand away, terror pooling in her belly as she reached for the call button on the bed.

"I wouldn't do that, Jenna." He spoke quietly, his silky voice shivering through her and adding to her terror.

"Who are you? What do you want?"

"I'm death, and I'm here to take what should have been mine a week ago." He grabbed the IV pole, shoved the syringe into the port.

Jenna screamed, yanking the needle from her arm, blood spurting from the wound as she leaped from the bed.

A fist closed around her hair, and she was yanked back, her head slamming into the wall as her attacker shoved her sideways. "You could have died easy, but I see that's not what you want."

"I don't want to die at all." She panted, stars bursting in front of her eyes, sharp pain exploding through her head. Would she lose her vision again? Would she have to fight blind?

Please, God, help me.

Please.

"Too bad. You make a deal with the devil and you end up going to—"

The bathroom door flew open, crashing against the wall as a man stumbled out. Tall, broad-shouldered.

Nikolai. Something dark and wet running down his face.

Blood.

A lot of it.

He grabbed the other man by the shirt, nearly lifting him from his feet as he swung him around and slammed a fist into his face. The guy stumbled back, bumping into the wall before righting himself, reaching behind his back, pulling something from beneath his shirt.

A knife.

He had a knife.

Nikolai grabbed the man's wrist, forcing his hand away, yelling for Jenna to run for help.

But she couldn't leave him there bleeding and fighting for his life. Couldn't run for help knowing that he might be dead before she returned. She slammed her finger onto the emergency call button, praying the nurses would come quickly. Then she lifted the plastic carafe of water, threw it into the face of her attacker.

He cursed, stumbling back.

Nikolai pounced, throwing himself straight at the man, at the knife, at certain death. Both men fell to the floor, wrestling for control of the knife, Nikolai struggling. Losing. Their attacker on top of him, the knife plunging toward Nikolai's heart, Nikolai barely managing to hold it away.

The door opened, and a nurse stepped in the room, turning on the light and letting out a shriek that must have carried down the hall. She screamed for security, her eyes wide with panic, and Jenna wanted to tell her to stop screaming and to start helping, but she was too busy struggling with what felt like three tons worth of IV pole. Too busy praying for a miracle of strength.

Finally, she managed to lift the pole, barely managed to swing it into the man who'd called himself death.

He tumbled sideways, the knife falling from his hand, then jumped up, trying to run to the door.

Nikolai grabbed his ankle, pulling him back down again.

Feet slapped against tile, people yelled for the hallway to be cleared.

"Freeze," a security guard commanded, pulling a gun from its holster as he entered the room.

And the whole world went silent.

"Both of you, put your hands up."

"I don't think that's a good idea. This guy tried to kill Jenna, and there is no way I'm going to give him the opportunity to try again." Nikolai pulled the man up by his shirt, shoving him toward the security guard, blood seeping down his temple in thick purplish rivulets.

"We need a doctor. My friend has been hurt," Jenna said, worry edging out fear.

"I'll be fine as long as this scum doesn't escape."

"No worries. We'll keep him handcuffed and under guard until the police arrive. Do you know him, ma'am?" the security guard asked as he frisked the guy.

"No." But she wished she did. At least then, she might have some clue as to why he'd tried to kill her.

"So, there's no bad blood between you? No reason that he'd want you dead?"

"She's breathing. That's enough reason for me," the man said, his dark gaze on Jenna. She shivered, and Nikolai wrapped an arm around her shoulder.

"Ignore him."

"I can't. I need to know why he's here. I need to know why he tried to kill me."

"Give me enough reason, and I just might tell you." The guy grinned, his eyes as cold and dead-looking as a snake's.

"I'll give you plenty," Nikolai said, stepping toward him, and Jenna grabbed the belt loop of his jeans.

"Let it go. It's the job of the police to question him. Not ours."

"The guy needs to be taught a lesson."

"But you won't be the one to do it. Unless you want to be

arrested, too," the security guard cut in, shoving the suspect to the door.

A cacophony of voices drifted into the room, and several police officers appeared, taking the man into custody and reading him his Miranda rights.

Officer Daniels stood behind them, scowling as he watched the guy being escorted away. "I was hoping we wouldn't be doing this again, but at least we've got someone in custody."

"That will only matter if you can find out why he was here." Nikolai walked to the door, cradling one arm against his chest as he stared down the hall.

"True, that. Looks like you got the worst of the fight this time, Jansen."

"The guy took out my arm with a wooden baton and then knocked me over the head."

"And he tried to stab you, Jenna?"

"No. He was going to shoot something into my IV. The syringe is on the ground somewhere."

"We'll collect it as evidence. See what was in it." He gestured for another officer to bag the syringe and the IV bag. "And maybe we'll get him to talk."

"The last guy didn't," Jenna said, wishing she were more confident of the outcome, more sure that this man's arrest would be the end of her nightmare.

"Yet. He may change his mind when he realizes how long he could be put away for." Officer Daniels's phone rang, and he glanced at the caller ID.

"If you'll excuse me for just a minute."

He took a few steps away, answering the call as a nurse approached Nikolai and began dabbing at the wound on his head.

"We need to bring you down to X-ray to get a look at your arm," the nurse said, and Nikolai shook his head.

"That's not going to happen. I'm staying here with Jenna until she's released."

"The police are right here, Nikolai. I'll be fine."

"I've stopped believing that. Until I know for sure that you're not going to be attacked again, I'm not going to leave your side."

"Quit being macho and go get the x-ray. You're not going to do me any good with a broken arm."

"I knew I could count on you to be supportive." Nikolai grinned, and Jenna smiled in return.

"Well, you *are* being macho."

"I'm being concerned. I don't know what I'd do if something happened to you." He grabbed her hand, twined his fingers through hers.

And she thought she could stay that way forever, the two of them connected in such a small way, the impact of it touching her to her very soul.

"Good news, folks." Officer Daniels shoved his phone back into his pocket, grinning widely. "That guy we just arrested? His name is Mack Stanley."

"The name doesn't sound familiar." And Jenna wasn't sure why having it was such good news.

"Maybe not to you. The guy has a rap sheet a mile long. He's wanted in two states for assault with a deadly weapon and there's a warrant out for his arrest in Austin. He's the prime suspect in a murder there. He's also known for stockpiling weapons. It wouldn't surprise me if we found World War II weapons in his cache."

"So you think he tossed the grenade this morning?"

"I don't know, but I'm going to find out."

"One way or another, he's not the kind of guy who should be out on the streets."

"No, but apparently he is the kind of guy who's got a healthy sense of self-preservation."

"What do you mean?" Nikolai leaned forward, his dark eyes alive with interest. How a guy who'd been knocked out, had his arm broken and nearly been killed could look so good, Jenna didn't know, but somehow, he managed it.

"It took him all of two minutes in the squad car to start singing like a jaybird."

"He's talking?"

"Yeah. And I think you can guess whose name he mentioned."

"John Romero's." Nikolai smiled.

"Bingo! Says Romero paid him $20,000 to get rid of Jenna. He got half up front and would have gotten the other half when she was dead. He says there's more that he can tell us, but he's not talking until he has a lawyer, and we offer him a deal. It's not much, but it's enough to bring Romero in for questioning."

"That's exactly what I wanted to hear." Nikolai tugged Jenna to his side, giving her a one-armed hug that heated her chilled skin.

John had hired someone to kill her.

Why? Did he blame her for Magdalena's death? Or was something else going on?

"You okay?" Nikolai's breath ruffled her hair as he spoke, his presence comforting and comfortable.

"I just want to know why John would do such a thing."

"That's what I'm going to ask him. If you two will excuse me, I'm going to meet John at the station and see what he has to say."

"He might deny it."

"He might, but since we found rat poison in the fire pit outside his house and remnants of it on the counter in the kitchen, I think it's safe to say, he's going to know that lying will do little good. I'll call you when I have more information. In the meantime, I think you can finally get back to your life, Jenna." Officer Daniels offered a brief wave and then retreated down the hall.

"Back to my life. I'm not even sure I know what that means."

"It means a little cottage in Washington and a cat named Dante warming your feet." Nikolai smiled gently as he stepped away, and Jenna wondered if it also included him or if he would slip back out of her life as quietly as he'd slipped into it.

She wanted to ask, but a doctor entered the room and urged Nikolai into a chair. Nurses closed in to offer supplies as his head wound was cleaned and stitched, and Jenna could do nothing but stand near the wall, watching, wondering.

Praying.

That she really *could* finally go back to her life.

That the nightmare she'd survived really *had* ended.

And that no matter what happened, no matter where she went from here, she'd be as content with her life as she had been before Nikolai entered it.

TWENTY-ONE

Life had a way of going on. No matter what the challenges. No matter what the problems. It continued, one moment, one hour, one experience at a time. Jenna had lived that truth many times. First during the years she'd spent fighting cancer, then during the past month's struggle. Three weeks after returning home, Jenna's time in Mexico and in Houston seemed like a bad dream. A bad dream that had ended with Magdalena dead and her husband in jail on charges of drug trafficking and attempted murder.

Jenna sighed, grabbing her Bible and heading out the door. Church would start in less than twenty minutes, and she didn't want to be late.

The beauty of the day, the pristine blue of the sky and the crisp, cool spring air did little to lift her spirit. She'd tried hard to get back into the swing of things. She'd gone back to work and Bible study. She'd sat through church services and been at the hospital when her sister-in-law had given birth to a beautiful baby girl.

But somehow she felt as if she were merely existing rather than living. No matter what she did, no matter where she went, she felt hollow and old, used up in some indefinable way.

Because you miss Nikolai.

The truth whispered through her mind, and she couldn't deny it. She'd spoken to him every day in the first two weeks after she'd left Houston. He'd needed pins put in his arm, and she'd spoken to him when he was groggy and fresh out of surgery. Her voice, he'd said, was the first one he'd wanted to hear. She'd believed him, believed that what had been forged in fire might actually survive.

And then the daily phone conversations had stopped. When they did speak, Nikolai sounded distracted and rushed, and Jenna had too much pride to ask him if he'd stopped caring.

She sighed, again. God was in control. He knew what was best. She had to trust in that and keep moving forward.

Even if that meant doing so alone.

Her cell phone rang as she got into her car, and her heart jumped, the hope that Nikolai might be calling swelling up and then crashing down again when she saw the number. "Hello?"

"Jenna, it's Officer Daniels. Sorry to call on a Sunday morning, but we've had a breakthrough in the case, and I wanted you to be the first to know."

"What's that?"

"John has agreed to a plea bargain. He's going to plead guilty to drug trafficking and attempted murder. We had enough evidence to bring him to trial for his wife's murder, and he's a savvy enough lawyer to know that he probably would have been convicted. The penalty for that would have been death. The penalty for attempted murder and drug trafficking amounts to a life sentence."

"I'm not sure how I feel about that."

"Feel good. We *could* have gotten the murder one conviction, and we *could* have sent him to death row, but sometimes things happen during trials, and I'd rather send him away on lesser charges than have him free because of reasonable doubt."

"I understand."

"I know it's not what you were hoping for."

"I wasn't hoping for anything. I just want to see justice done."

"It will be."

"Not if he doesn't admit that he had Magdalena murdered for her trust money."

"He's still maintaining that she died because she got in the Panthers' way. John shipped the money the same way he'd done a half dozen times before. A quarter of a million dollars hidden in false bottoms in several of the medical supply crates. Members of the Panthers were supposed to retrieve the money and then arrange for transport of cocaine into the States."

"But Magdalena caught them removing the money." Jenna had heard the story before, and each time she wondered how she hadn't known what was going on in those first few days in Mexico.

"She thought they were stealing supplies and she contacted the police, and then put the supplies under heavy guard. The Panthers weren't happy to have their plans interfered with, and they meted out her punishment. Unfortunately, you got caught in the crossfire, and ended up being kidnapped with your friend."

That much, at least, rang true with what Jenna remembered. When the door to the hotel crashed in, the men who'd entered had grabbed Magdalena. It wasn't until Jenna tried to intervene that she was thrown into the van with her friend. "I still don't know why they let me live."

"Crazy as it seems, the Panthers do have a code of ethics. They only kill those who interfere with their organization."

"And people they're paid to get rid of?"

"If those people are deemed a threat."

"And, I'm sure John could easily have made it seem as if Magdalena was."

"I agree, but it's difficult to prove."

"I know."

"I really am sorry, Jenna. I know you were hoping he'd be tried for murder one."

"You've done everything you can. I know that."

"I only wish I would have done more sooner. John had a

good reputation as a defense attorney. He knew how to keep his finances in order even as he gambled away hundreds of thousands of dollars. On the surface, he looked great. It wasn't until we started digging deeper that we realized he had serious problems with some seriously bad people. He owed money to men who were getting impatient to be paid."

"And poor Magdalena had plenty of money in the trust her parents left her."

"That doesn't mean he had her killed to gain access to it."

"Maybe not, but it's very convenient that she died just when John most needed money."

"Like I said before, I agree. The fact is, I believe that if he'd known you'd been named trustee of Benjamin's inheritance *before* Magdalena died, you never would have made it out of Mexico alive."

The words were a chilling reminder of just how close Jenna had come to death. She shivered, cranking up the heat in the car. "Thanks. I needed a few more nightmares to add to my collection."

"Sorry. How about I make it up to you by having you over to dinner the next time you're in town? My wife fries a mean chicken, and her pecan pie is—"

"Please don't say 'to die for.'"

He chuckled, and Jenna relaxed for the first time since she'd answered the phone.

"I was going to say 'the best I've ever had.'"

"In that case, I'd love to come, but I doubt I'll be back in Houston anytime soon. Since John's parents took Benjamin to their place in California, I really don't have any reason to visit there." John's parents had had no part in their son's crimes and were devastated by his arrest. They'd left Houston soon after Jenna and were eager to build a strong relationship with her for the sake of their grandson.

"I thought you and Jansen were an item."

So had she, but she didn't say that to Officer Daniels

"We're friends. I hate to cut the conversation short, but I have to get to church."

"I'll call you if things change."

"Thanks." She pulled onto the road, wanting to put everything behind her and go on stronger and better for what she'd been through.

Determined to put everything behind her and go on.

She liked that word better, liked the strength of it.

God had brought her through so much, and she wasn't going sit around and mope because Nikolai had left a hole in her life.

And in her heart.

She frowned, pulling into the church parking lot and getting out of the car. Several people were walking into church ahead of her, and she held back, waiting until they entered the building. As much as she loved her church family, she was getting tired of telling her story. To everyone else, what had happened seemed terrifying and exotic and exciting. To Jenna it was a memory that haunted her dreams and her nightmares.

"Jen?" A voice called out from across the parking lot, and Jenna turned, her heart leaping as she saw a familiar figure jogging toward her.

"Nikolai?"

"Who else?" He stopped in front of her, his right arm in a sling, his face handsome and rugged and so very welcome it took Jenna's breath away.

"How did you find me here?"

"I called your brother when I got into town and asked where you'd be. He sent me here."

"You could have called me."

"I wanted to surprise you. Hopefully, it's a pleasant one." He grinned, and the hollowness inside Jenna filled with joy and relief and the first sweet bloom of love.

"It's the best surprise I've had in years," she said, wrapping her arms around his waist and hugging him tight, inhaling mint and masculinity and the subtle compelling scent that was Nikolai.

"I've got a better one."

"What?"

"I'm renting a place just a few miles from your house. I finalized the details on Monday, packed my things and headed this way."

Surprised, she leaned back and looked up into his face. "Is *that* why you haven't called?"

"Did you think there was some other reason?"

"I..."

"What?" He pulled her close again, burying his face in her hair, his lips finding the tender spot behind her ear.

She shivered, no longer sure what they were talking about. No longer caring.

"You feel so good. Every time I'm in your arms, I feel like I'm home," she whispered, and he chuckled.

"Does that mean you missed me?" He looked into her face, his deep brown eyes filled with humor and warmth.

"Maybe."

"Just maybe?"

"Okay. Definitely. But I still think you should have told me you were moving here."

"If you're going to tell me that I shouldn't have come, don't bother."

"Why would I?"

"Because you don't trust in what you feel for me, and you're afraid that what we have won't last."

"Maybe I am, but I've realized you were right. I can't just sit around twiddling my thumbs while life passes me by. I need to go after what I want."

"And what is it that you want?"

"You." She took his hand, pressing a kiss to his palm as she looked into his eyes, saw her future written clearly there.

"Then, what are we waiting for?" he asked, twining his

fingers with hers as he started walking toward the church. "Let's get started on forever."

At his words, Jenna's heart swelled with a love so strong and real that she couldn't deny it. "There's only one thing you forgot, Nikolai."

"What's that?"

"This." She pulled his head down for a kiss filled with promises of a million tomorrows spent together, a million dreams fulfilled.

He wrapped his good arm around her waist, deepening the kiss, adding his own promises to hers until there was nothing but the future spinning out in front of them, beckoning them to whatever God had planned.

* * * * *

Dear Reader,

Life isn't perfect, and being a Christian doesn't save us from going through trials. Jenna Dougherty experiences this first-hand when she is diagnosed with leukemia. After battling the disease for two years, she's finally in remission. Determined to live life to the fullest, she agrees to take part in a medical mission trip to Mexico. She expects the trip to be exciting and fulfilling. Instead, she is kidnapped and blinded. Her struggle to hold on to faith during such trying circumstances reflects the struggles many of us experience. Though we understand that God is God even in the tough times, we are often filled with worry and fear. I hope that as you read *Running Blind*, you will be challenged to trust more fully in God's power and grace, and I pray that you will always know the fullness of His love and faithfulness.

As always, I love to hear from readers. If you have time, drop me a line at shirlee@shirleemccoy.com.

Blessings,

Shirlee McCoy

QUESTIONS FOR DISCUSSION

1. Jenna Dougherty has survived cancer only to be thrown into another life-and-death struggle. Is her faith strengthened by her struggles? Or is it shaken?

2. As Christians, we are not immune to troubles and trials. What scripture verses do you cling to during troubling times?

3. Have there been times when your faith has floundered? If so, what helped buoy you up and keep you focused on the truth of God's power and faithfulness?

4. Nikolai's background is filled with heartache and loss. How has that shaped him as a person?

5. How would you describe Nikolai's faith? Do you think it is difficult or easy for him to allow God to have control of his life?

6. Jenna used to dream of getting married and having children. What has happened to make her believe that her dream will never come true?

7. Do you think that her infertility is a good reason for closing herself off to the idea of marriage, or is it simply an excuse she uses to keep from getting hurt again?

8. It's obvious that Jenna's dreams were not God's dreams for her life. Have there been times when you've pursued a dream only to find that God has other plans?

9. How does aligning our dreams with God's lead to fulfillment?

10. What dreams does Nikolai have for his life?

11. Jenna and Nikolai both have survivor's guilt. How does that impact their relationship?

12. How does Jenna deal with Magdalena's death? Does faith ease the sting of the loss?

13. What is it about Nikolai that makes Jenna want to lean on him? Why is she so determined not to?

14. Painful relationships can burden our hearts and keep us from enjoying all that God has planned for us. Are your past relationships hurting current ones?

15. What steps are important to true healing when it comes to broken relationships?

16. Have you been willing to forgive and move on? If so, how has that changed your life?

Love Inspired
SUSPENSE

TITLES AVAILABLE NEXT MONTH

Available December 7, 2010

CHRISTMAS BODYGUARD
Guardians, Inc.
Margaret Daley

THE SOLDIER'S MISSION
Lenora Worth

NIGHT PREY
Sharon Dunn

YULETIDE DEFENDER
Sandra Robbins

LISCNM1110

REQUEST YOUR FREE BOOKS!
2 FREE RIVETING INSPIRATIONAL NOVELS
PLUS 2 FREE MYSTERY GIFTS

YES! Please send me 2 FREE Love Inspired® Suspense novels and my 2 FREE mystery gifts (gifts are worth about $10). After receiving them, if I don't wish to receive any more books, I can return the shipping statement marked "cancel". If I don't cancel, I will receive 4 brand-new novels every month and be billed just $4.24 per book in the U.S. or $4.74 per book in Canada. That's a saving of 20% off the cover price. It's quite a bargain! Shipping and handling is just 50¢ per book.* I understand that accepting the 2 free books and gifts places me under no obligation to buy anything. I can always return a shipment and cancel at any time. Even if I never buy another book, the two free books and gifts are mine to keep forever.

123/323 IDN E7QZ

Name	(PLEASE PRINT)	
Address		Apt. #
City	State/Prov.	Zip/Postal Code

Signature (if under 18, a parent or guardian must sign)

Mail to Steeple Hill Reader Service:
IN U.S.A.: P.O. Box 1867, Buffalo, NY 14240-1867
IN CANADA: P.O. Box 609, Fort Erie, Ontario L2A 5X3

Not valid for current subscribers to Love Inspired Suspense books.

Want to try two free books from another series?
Call 1-800-873-8635 or visit www.morefreebooks.com.

* Terms and prices subject to change without notice. Prices do not include applicable taxes. Sales tax applicable in N.Y. Canadian residents will be charged applicable provincial taxes and GST. Offer not valid in Quebec. This offer is limited to one order per household. All orders subject to approval. Credit or debit balances in a customer's account(s) may be offset by any other outstanding balance owed by or to the customer. Please allow 4 to 6 weeks for delivery. Offer available while quantities last.

Your Privacy: Steeple Hill Books is committed to protecting your privacy. Our Privacy Policy is available online at www.SteepleHill.com or upon request from the Reader Service. From time to time we make our lists of customers available to reputable third parties who may have a product or service of interest to you. If you would prefer we not share your name and address, please check here. ☐

Help us get it right—We strive for accurate, respectful and relevant communications. To clarify or modify your communication preferences, visit us at www.ReaderService.com/consumerschoice.

LISUS10R

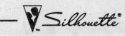

SPECIAL EDITION

USA TODAY BESTSELLING AUTHOR

MARIE FERRARELLA

BRINGS YOU ANOTHER
HEARTWARMING STORY FROM

When Lilli McCall disappeared on him
after he proposed, Kullen Manetti swore
never to fall in love again. Eight years later
Lilli is back in his life, threatening to break
down all the walls he's put up to
safeguard his heart.

UNWRAPPING
THE PLAYBOY

*Available December
wherever books are sold.*